Looking Through
the
Rear Window

Noreen Reeves

This book is dedicated to
Connie Falkiner
1948 – 2002

Contents

Introduction

"Life isn't about finding yourself or finding anything — it's about creating yourself."
Bob Dylan[1]

All of us have a story. Many of us have been told, you should write a book because sometimes a real-life story can be funnier, more exciting, sadder, scarier, or happier than real-life.

Following the wonderful feedback I received for my memoir, *Two Shakes of a Dead Lamb's Tail,* I was encouraged to follow it up with another book featuring stories of my life and the sometimes crazy situations I have found myself in.

Looking Through the Rear Window is a compilation of some of those situations and also includes some fictitious tales.

Enjoy!

Noreen Reeves
2019

---

[1] Quote originally attributed to George Bernard Shaw.

Vancouver Airport

In August 2011, a friend and I visited Canada for a holiday. We flew Perth-Sydney-Vancouver, arriving in the late morning just in time to board the *MS Volendam*, for Alaska. The long queue through US Customs, and Border Protection was sorely testing many people's patience. Eventually we walked out into rays of cool, weak sunshine, finally able to feel like we could relax after the very long flight.

We spent nine days on this fabulous ship, sailing through the Inside Passage to Skagway. I'm not sure why, but the intrigue of Skagway has always been one destination that I was keen to visit. I wasn't disappointed. Many of the flat-fronted two-storey brightly coloured buildings were timber originals and were the epitome of what you see in cowboy movies, with high-stepped wooden verandas. My imagination was rampant with images of bygone days. The only items missing were the hitching rails and the dusty dirt roads.

Although I'm not mad about cruises, I have to admit that when the nine days were up, my friend and I were not keen to disembark. The ambience on the ship was relaxing and pleasurable, and the cuisine was outstanding. We visited glaciers both by sea and helicopter, walking the terrain and finding our ice legs – skirting crevasses and experiencing a northern summer, rugged up to the nines in warm protective clothing.

Having navigated the plethora of Vancouver street-beggars we eventually found the bus that would take us to Whistler, to visit my friend's daughter. After five hot days in the very picturesque Whistler Valley we returned to Vancouver and boarded the *Rocky Mountaineer*. The spectacular scenery and engaging towns and lakes that were visited along the way left us awestruck. After a breathtaking helicopter ride over the Rockies we ended this part of our journey in Calgary. Three days later we flew to Vancouver for the return trip home. Neither of us was looking forward to the long Air Canada flight that was unavoidable and inevitable.

We arrived at the international airport with the expectation that our return flight to Sydney would depart at 11.00 pm. The boarding lounge slowly began to fill with fellow passengers, some wandering around just to keep mobile, while children made the most of the available free time to burn off stored energy.

Eleven pm came and went. Everyone had been watching the clocks and flight monitors for some time, expecting an announcement, but none was forthcoming. Eleven forty-five passed and the desultory passengers began to fidget, myself included. The delay was frustrating. At approximately 12.30 am Air Canada made the announcement that our flight was late because the plane we were to board was coming from Toronto, a six-hour flight away. They would keep us posted. The collective agitation was rife.

The Toronto plane landed at 1.00 am. However, there was a mechanical problem and we were advised the crew and ground staff were working as fast as they could to resolve the issue. But who wants to board a plane for a 14-hour flight, over water, if there is a problem? The frustrated seat shuffling-cum-muttering escalated.

At 2.30 am we were advised that because of the plane's late arrival, the aircrew were now out of time. Air Canada would have to fly in another crew to take their place. The plane apparently could not be repaired quickly enough by the time the new crew arrived, so we would be bussed to hotels to spend the night. Could we please queue up at the counter to receive our bus tickets. Anyone wishing to remain at the airport could do so and blankets and pillows would be supplied.

In hindsight this would have probably been the better option, but if we had stayed at the airport this story would never have been written, as we would have missed one of the most hilarious, entertaining, frightening and unbelievable episodes in ridiculous human behaviour.

There was a stampede to the counter with tired passengers pushing and manoeuvring, trying to be closest to the front of the queue. All you could do was stand in line and hold your place to the best of your ability, as queue-jumpers angled to gain the foremost positions. Tickets were dispensed and we made our way outside through the crisp, frosty night air to the waiting coaches. Being almost last to board, we had to stand. Parents with pushers were squashed into any available space while gripping their children and struggling to keep a hold on their hand luggage.

The bus was dreadfully overcrowded but there was little anyone could do. Everyone was tired and frustrated. The sooner the hotel was reached, the better. To add tension to the mix, there were six loud young Australian men, all seated – not being gentlemanly enough to offer their seats to parents or the elderly, and one of them had the cough from hell. He sounded like a barking seal – and it was a very loud bark. In between the talk and chatter, this *bark* would erupt and everyone in close vicinity would consciously turn away, hoping to avoid contamination.

The overcrowded bus lurched off and twenty minutes later we arrived at a hotel. The time was now approximately 3.15 am. Those of us who were lucky enough to be standing were first off and there was a rush to get inside out of the cold, get away from the *bark* and be close to first in line at the counter. The Hotel Manager was doing his best to guide people through the foyer, attempting to keep everyone in an orderly line. Three young ladies were processing people's passports and identification with the view to allocating them a room.

The process was painstakingly slow and people's agitation was at its peak. This night had turned into a disaster and all anyone wanted was a room and a bed. Approximately half-a-dozen people had been processed and disappeared into the lifts. Lucky them! The next in line was an American family of five who moved to the left-hand side of the counter. The female in this group was a very loud woman who seemed intent on keeping the whole foyer informed of any issue that came to the fore. Being solidly built and with a grating voice, it was fairly obvious to everyone that she wore the pants.

Without warning, four burly Canadian cops burst through a side door with the officer in charge screaming into his shoulder radio, "Get that guy in the red shirt, get that guy in the red shirt, the guy at the back of the line, get the guy in the red shirt!" Everyone stood paralysed. This happened so quickly and unexpectedly we were all in a mild state of shock. Who was the guy in the red shirt and what had he done? Like puppets on a string, everyone turned in unison to try and comprehend the issue.

As the centre counter spot was vacated, two elderly ladies stepped up to the desk. The woman next in line, who was in front of us was an African, with the cutest little two-year-old who was doing her best to hold it together, given the very late hour. We were rather pleased we were one slot away from the counter, but our quiet elation was suddenly destroyed. The elderly lady at the middle counter and closest to the American family suddenly collapsed sideways in a dead faint, falling into the loud American Momma. The whole place suddenly turned into chaos.

American Momma went into screaming overdrive. The Hotel Manager appeared out of nowhere. The *red shirt* cops came roaring back through the same side door they had previously entered and the counter processing ceased, all in a matter of seconds. Mayhem ensued! American Momma was on her knees yelling, "I've got her pulse, I've got her pulse, I'm tellin' ya I've got her pulse." Someone was phoning the ambulance. The biggest burliest cop was trying to push American Momma aside, who weighed almost as much as he did. The queue disintegrated. Everyone was trying to do something without anybody quite knowing what had to be done.

Fortunately, after ten minutes of complete carnage, some order reigned. The elderly lady who was still on her feet was finally processed, as was the African and her little girl. They hastily disappeared to the lifts and my friend and I were beckoned forward. Meanwhile, the Fire Brigade had arrived with a defibrillator. American Momma was still telling anyone who would listen, "I'm tellin' ya, I got her pulse, I got her pulse, it was forty-four. I'm tellin' ya I got her pulse", her overpowering voice ricocheting off the walls. From what I observed, I think because Momma had *got her pulse* she felt this gave her *rights* over the prone body. Fortunately, the elderly woman had regained semiconsciousness, although she was obviously dazed and confused. The ambulance and paramedics finally arrived and thankfully took control, tactfully putting Momma in her place.

My friend and I headed for the lifts, thankful all the excitement was done. But not quite! The lift doors opened divulging the elderly lady and the African with her little girl, both women almost hysterical. The elderly lady with her bag and the African lady with her bag, the pusher and the little girl, were all that seemingly could fit in the lift. Amazed that they were still there, we asked what was the issue? With that the lift doors closed. My friend hastily pushed the up button. The doors reopened. The women frantically tried to explain that the lift wouldn't work and they couldn't get to their rooms.

Doors closing.

As the doors reopened someone ran up behind us and explained that the room card had to be swiped for the lift to work.

Doors closing!

Doors opening.

My friend and I forced our way into the tiny lift, which wasn't easy as we also had small backpacks.

Doors closing.

Five squashed people reshuffled into the tight space. The cute little African child's face was wet with tears. Who could blame her, but not one sound did she emit. The distress in that lift was profound.

The key card was swiped and we headed skywards! Fortunately, we were all on the same floor. Disembarking at level three we stood there in dismay. The corridors issued forth like ragged octopus tentacles, running every which way. The elderly lady threw her hands in the air and for a moment I thought she was going to collapse. I took one look at the African whose eyes had glazed over and knew it was time to step up. All thoughts of having a shower and going to bed disappeared. My friend and I checked the room numbers on the corridors and then checked the ladies' room numbers on their cards. I took the African by the arm and gently guided her to the right, leaving my friend to take care of the elderly woman. The length of these meandering corridors was like traversing a football field. The African woman's room was at the far end of corridor 'right'. I slipped the key card in the door, pushed it open and pulled her in. She just stood there, totally vacant. I turned on the lights and asked her what I could do. She just looked at me saying, "It ok, it ok." Not wanting to bolt I reassured her that she was safe, that we had to be at the airport this same morning by 9.00 am. "It ok." I closed the door and ran back towards the lifts, only to find my friend and the elderly lady, still hunting for her room in the middle corridor. Voila! The door to this room was tucked in behind a recess that was difficult to see, right outside the lifts. Once found, she hastily explained that she and the lady who had collapsed had travelled together from Toronto earlier that day. Neither of them had eaten or had anything to drink since breakfast the previous morning. She thanked us profusely and shut the door.

Corridor 'left' was our retreat and another football field was traversed, which had us in the very end room. After hasty showers and brushed teeth we fell into bed. It was now 4.00 am and breakfast was at seven! The second my head hit the pillow I was asleep. The alarm rang at 6.30 am and we struggled out, both looking like 'the hard day's night' was still in progress. We found the dining room that was already quite full and took a seat. Air Canada had *generously* given us a breakfast voucher, which covered tea or coffee and two slices of toast! We were just settling into our seats when the *bark* began at the table next to ours. I thought my friend was going to scream!

At 9.00 am we returned to the airport for an 11.00 am departure. Expectations were at a premium. Eleven am came and went. There was still no announcement. This may be fanciful thinking on my part, but I do believe someone must have complained at the Air Canada desk because suddenly there was a flurry of activity. Announcements were made to the effect that because we were now over twelve hours behind schedule, connecting flights had been rebooked and the information regarding same would be divulged closer to our destination.

Finally, at 1.00 pm we departed Vancouver and I don't think I've ever been so pleased to step onto a plane. The flight was long and arduous. The cabin crew were more interested in staff camaraderie than dispensing goodwill and bonhomie to the tired, overwrought passengers. As we neared Sydney, we were advised anyone connecting to Melbourne would disembark first as their forward flight was waiting. Those of us travelling to other states would be taken to a hotel for the night and would catch a flight home the following day.

We just looked at each other. What would this night bring?

I Don't Remember

In 2018 I made a trip to Victoria and travelled over much of the state by train to catch up with friends and family. I was now on the last leg of my journey, training it to Mentone where I was to meet up with my youngest son Dylan and stay the night with him and his family. He was taking me to Tullamarine the following morning to catch my return flight to Perth.

I have sometimes pondered that I must have something written on my forehead, invisible to me but obvious to other people, especially a certain type of man. I always seem to attract various individuals who insist on starting a conversation, uninvited. Some of this is understandable, as at markets where I am selling my book, men are attracted by the title and the fact that sheep are involved. Some of their conversations were truly interesting as they have shorn sheep, owned sheep or been involved with farming. On the other hand, if they have read some of the reviews that friends have kindly given, they notice that I once lived in New Guinea and that they had worked somewhere in PNG also. Swapping information regarding having lived there is always interesting.

However, some people wishing to engage me in so-called conversations often results in them giving an overextended blurb of their life and how interesting they and their work are. On these occasions after some time has elapsed, I usually try to extricate myself either pleading with a friend to save me or excusing myself, saying I badly need to pee!

***

Back to the train trip! I boarded the train at Southern Cross Station, having just spent a couple of hours with my friend Dot, who had travelled down from Broadford. We had worked together in our late teens and hadn't seen each other for fifty years!

Given it was early afternoon the train was almost devoid of passengers. Because I had a small suitcase and don't like crowds, I manoeuvred the case down the carriage and managed to find four spare seats facing each other. Pushing the suitcase over to the window, I sat down in the aisle seat and relaxed. I was looking forward to seeing parts of Melbourne I had not visited for many years.

The next stop was Flinders Street. A few people disembarked and others boarded. An older teenager sat on an opposite aisle seat and immediately immersed himself in his phone. As I was busy 'people watching', a passenger came from the door behind and plonked himself down directly opposite.

Of all the empty seats in the carriage, my space was suddenly invaded by a very tall, elderly man (his hairy knees were almost touching mine as he sat), wearing a pair of baggy shorts, a red T-shirt with white writing, a peak cap and a gold stud in his left ear. Aged wrinkles accentuated the chiselled crags of his face and he had a wide mouth that looked like pockmarked corrugated iron, which rippled when he spoke. I tried very hard not to look, but when you are so invaded in what was really a large space, given the number of empty seats, it was impossible to ignore him. I almost expostulated, *did you really have to sit here?* Then I thought of my forehead and what was invisibly written there!

"Gidday."

I smiled a weak, shallow smile. "Hullo."

10

"Nice day."

"Yes, it is rather," although that's not what I felt like saying.

"Where you off to then?"

I gave a short explanation.

"Ahh! So where ya from?"

"WA."

"Oh jeez, I lived there years ago. I lived in Floreat and other parts of Perth for about fourteen years."

"Oh, really."

"Yeah. Nice place Perth."

I then got some history on how he'd been a shearer and worked here, there and everywhere. It was obvious I wasn't going to escape and inwardly succumbed to the hope his disembarkation was imminent.

In some ways I probably do this man an injustice. He was obviously a people person and just wanted to chat, but given the number of empty seats, why choose me? In the process we exchanged stories about farming and animals and how young people today mostly have no idea of what it's like growing up on the land. What it's like to go without! We also chatted about shooting and skinning bunnies and how good rabbit is to eat.

Surreptitiously observing the young bloke sitting opposite, I realised he had obviously become aware of our conversation and some of the exchanged humour. I could tell his phone wasn't nearly as fascinating as what he was hearing, especially about gutting and skinning bunnies. I even saw him try to stifle the odd smile.

Stations came and stations went and I was beginning to think that my companion was there for the long haul when suddenly, out of the blue he said, "Whaddaya doin' tonight? There's this rock 'n roll concert on in Dandenong and I was wonderin' if you would like to come with me? It'll be a really good night. All the sixties and seventies music, dancin' and havin' the odd beer. Should be fun!"

Now I admit the train was making the usual squeaking, clattering train noises but I confess that for a moment I didn't think I'd heard right and almost stopped breathing. In trying to collect myself I wasn't sure if he had a short-term memory or that he had completely missed the bit about me spending my last night at my son's.

I spluttered while trying to collect myself. With a forced smile I thanked him for his invitation but reiterated that I was departing the next morning, early.

"Ah, yeah! Sorry. Ya did say that. Shame tho', it woulda been good."

I gave one of my sunny smiles and replied, "Well, maybe next time!"

"OK. This is me comin' up. Nice meetin' ya. Safe trip luv!"

"Thank you."

As the train gathered speed I couldn't help but smile at the thought of what Dylan would have said if I'd told him I'd had a *better* offer!

Later, on musing over this funny little episode I thought my departed companion said his name was George, but I don't remember!

My Best Friend's Funeral

Despair. The overriding emotion I felt when I learnt of my best friend Connie's fate. Having been diagnosed with a pernicious abdominal cancer, sadly, she passed away on 12 April 2002.

Connie spent her last Christmas in Perth with me and she phoned a month later to tell me her time was drawing close. After sharing long distance tears, both of us had to face the soul-searching resignation and reality of the tenuous hold we all have on life. More particularly because of the one that was about to be cut short. She was just 54.

Most days over that Christmas period she would wander down to the local beach at Scarborough, tuck herself into a protective sand dune crevice out of the capricious breeze and either read a book or just sit and ponder. No doubt the ebb and flow of the waves reflected her innermost emotions as she contemplated her lot. She may have even been praying for preternatural intervention, to placate the overwhelming anguish she no doubt felt regarding her impending fate.

I had known her for years and knew that her childhood was not the happiest but she had never divulged her deepest regrets and sorrows. I suspect the deep-seated cancer was the insidious result of holding on to a great deal of anger, antagonism and resentment, being unable, as a child, to voice the anguish of the shattering experience of losing her dearly beloved father.

Having lived in South Africa and Madagascar as a young and carefree nursing sister, Connie had an almost insatiable love affair with the Indian Ocean. Her thin, tired voice came down the line.

"When I'm gone there's something I'd like you to do. I want you to spread my ashes in the ocean at Scarborough. You know where I liked to sit. Just go down to the shallows and throw them in."

"No way Jose! The waves there can be substantial and with so much power behind them you'll end up all over the beach."

"It won't matter."

"Yes it will! Some poor bugger will be sitting on the sand with you all over them. I'm not having that!"

As her time grew near my husband and I drove hastily across the Nullabor. Three days later, we rang Tim (Connie's husband) to let him know we were on our way. He advised Connie had taken a turn for the worse and had been moved to Leongatha hospital in South Gippsland. Tim suggested we bypass Melbourne and head straight for the hospital. The situation was grim.

We arrived in the late afternoon and were quietly shown into a large private room where Connie lay. A reclining armchair in one corner covered with pastel-coloured blankets was where Tim slept each night, keeping vigil. A large double window facilitated the sunshine to stream through pink hibiscus onto Connie's bed enabling dappled shadows to dance on the covers, shedding some small, warm comfort to a sad and difficult situation. Connie rallied enough strength to give us a wan, tired smile. It broke my heart to see my friend in this stricken state. We hugged and smiled through teary eyes and managed to have a stilted conversation about our trip and how lovely it was to see her.

John and I spent a contented half-hour there, reliving some of our shared, funny moments, such as sitting on the back of her nephew's tractor on freezing, frosty mornings on the Lindenow flats, planting broccoli and cabbages and solving the world's problems.

It wasn't nearly long enough, but the effort for her to stay focused proved difficult. Furthermore, the emotional situation was taking its toll on me. I could feel myself plummeting. Giving her one last loving hug I hurried from the room. My heart was breaking. John sat with her for another five minutes, holding her hand, quietly saying goodbye. Tim told us afterwards that our visit had made a difference. He hadn't seen her so bright and animated for quite some time. This news was cold comfort as her deterioration was palpable. Connie passed away ten days later. Thinking of Connie now, I'm grateful we were able to bring a little sunshine into her ravaged but beautiful heart.

Six months later I flew to Victoria to collect her ashes from Tim. A friend in Melbourne, Kerry, kindly offered to drive me to the airport. Connie's urn was enclosed in a box with some of her personal effects. As my luggage and the box were being checked through security, the officer enquired about the package.

"What's in the box?" Before I could answer he said, "I hope it's nothing incendiary?" I was taken aback but it brought a not-so-stifled snigger from Kerry.

"Ah", said Kerry, "I wouldn't exactly say it was incendiary. It's a bit late for that!"

"Why, what do you mean?" he asked, his inquisitorial antennae on immediate alert.

I sadly replied, "It's my best friend's ashes." He dropped the box as though it were a hot potato and stood there looking dismayed.

"It's ok", I said, "I promise it won't blow up!"

Back in Perth with my precious cargo, the next task was to find a suitable place to keep the urn. I wanted somewhere *comfortable*. Sliding the box into a colourful tapestry bag that Connie had made, I placed it behind my stand-alone oak mirror in the corner of our bedroom. John and the kids all agreed to be part of the spreading ceremony. They were all very fond of 'our Con!' The date was set for Sunday 16 February 2003.

The day dawned overcast and humid. Our eldest son Andrew lived in Bunbury and was therefore too far away to make the trip to Perth. Dylan had just arrived home from Nepal and Thailand where he had been a Group Leader as part of the Duke of Edinburgh Award. His timing was excellent. Melanie, our daughter, was to accompany us but her back was giving her trouble, so John, Dylan and I set off to catch the 8.40 am ferry from Fremantle. Rottnest Island sits twenty-five kilometres off the coast of Perth surrounded by the magnificent Indian Ocean. This is where we decided to spread Connie's ashes.

I was feeling extremely emotional. Connie had been tucked up in the colourful bag in our bedroom for several months and I didn't want to part with her, but I'd made a promise and the time had come to say a proper farewell.

Menacing black clouds sitting in conjunction with the horizon loomed like some prehistoric dragon.

Forked lightning intermittently rent the sky, yet the crossing to the island was unexpectedly smooth given what appeared to be an approaching calamity. I had misgivings but put it down to the emotion of the moment. We intended to hire a small craft and sail offshore. I had bought some delicate blood-red roses coupled with eucalyptus leaves and pink thryptomene to throw in the water after the ashes were spread. A small psychological battle was raging within as I knew I was going to have difficulty performing this act. It was all about letting go, that, at the time, was not one of my strengths!

Once ashore we made our way to the Information Shop and took our place in the rapidly growing queue, only to be told sorry, boats can't be hired, however, small motorised craft are available at Geordie Bay. We took an information leaflet, complete with map and headed for the free transit bus. Unfortunately it was heading for the airstrip in the opposite direction. It would be back in half-an-hour. The two km walk was looking good. Craving the exercise, the walk, with luck, would help soothe my angst.

A stiff breeze was blowing and it was overcast. Crossing a low sandy depression, we weren't able to see the water or the proximity of the oncoming storm. Intent on our mission, we pressed on. Ten minutes into the walk I suddenly remembered I didn't have any film. Distraught, as I'd promised Tim I would take photos, we returned to the shop. We then headed for the transit bus as it was due. After this small stuff-up, we didn't want any more hiccups.

The dusty red bus arrived and the fifteen-minute trip was memorably uneventful. Disinterested passengers with oversized floppy hats and wearing an assortment of shabby casual clothes embarked or disembarked at will. My tension was rising. Everything about me seemed to be highly illuminated. Even the small dust particles on the seat of the bus seemed magnified, as though someone had covered the vinyl in fine gravel.

Geordie Bay is a small picturesque inlet on the northern side of the island, comprising several mustard-coloured holiday villas which overlooked the many and varied yachts and boats anchored offshore. We joined the craft queue, squinting from the glare of the fractured light that bounced off the now choppy water. The craft were two-seaters with a small overhead canopy and a clear perspex front for observing fish swimming below. The cost was $15 for half-an-hour. "Thanks, we'll take two." Burley (pellets) was supplied to feed the fish.

As we wanted to keep our real purpose private we took the burley and climbed into our craft with Dylan in one, and John and me in the other. Instructions were given on the gears, forward and reverse. Boundaries to observe were delineated. The timer was set for half-an-hour and Dylan was away. The wind heightened beyond stiff breeze capacity and the choppy waves slapped noisily against the sides of the craft. Thick pewter-coloured clouds scudded swiftly towards us as though picking their targets. The wind doubled in velocity. Large cold wet globules of rain began belting into us, sideways. Our little craft chugged and struggled to maintain a course that would take us away from the anchored yachts. With the water slap-slap-slapping the sides of the craft – intermittently flaying us with flecks of fat foam, the choppy sea churned us like a slow spinning top. We were in fifth gear going nowhere thanks to the wind. Meanwhile Dylan, being in complete control of his craft, raced ahead like a Formula 1 driver. Everything was going just swimmingly for him!

We ploughed into the wind and rain trying to avoid the moored craft, when suddenly the gear stick came unstuck. John and I were drifting helplessly, bobbing around like corks in a bottle with a bewildered Dylan looking back at us wondering what we were doing. There was much cursing and swearing as the chilly, wet drops of rain splattered over our exposed flesh and thin clothing. Dylan turned and came skimming across the waves towards us with the wind willingly shooing him along. At that moment some divine intervention transpired. 'Thanks Connie – you were a bit early with the trauma!'

John managed to wiggle and jiggle the gear stick back into position. We were again mobile. Reaching the other side of the bay was heavy going but finally we were out of sight of the shore and could begin our little ceremony.

I suddenly realised I hadn't put the film in the camera – and Dylan had my bag. He attempted to manoeuvre between the anchored yachts and us, with the choppy sea slapping and slopping all over us in a most perfunctory manner. I had visions of the backpack going overboard during the exchange. What a time to play 'pass the parcel'! Incredibly the transition went relatively smoothly, but then I couldn't find the camera. Out came the contents of the bag while John and Dylan desperately tried to keep the two craft together. I cursed my stupidity and lack of diligence in not having the camera already loaded. Fumbling frantically while trying to balance the rest of the paraphernalia in my lap, I suddenly felt old!

With the camera successfully loaded, I began grappling with the parcel that contained Connie's urn. The wind was relentless. The sea was on the boil, no thanks to the direction of the wind. The rain was soaking us to the bone. The blokes battled the elements to keep the two craft close together. Dylan kept turning in circles while it was all John could do to keep us upright. Off came the brown paper that was wrapped around the card board container holding the urn, which was the size of a large brick. The box was stapled to the max! And taped! Bloody hell!

"Who's got a knife?"

Dylan began drifting away.

"Why didn't you open this before we left home?"

"I couldn't. I knew I was going to find this hard and I just didn't feel capable of unwrapping it beforehand. I didn't realise it was going to be this complicated."

We didn't have a knife!

John asked for the car keys.

"I don't have them."

"Yes you do."

"No I don't. You locked the car back at the wharf and kept the keys."

John fumbled in his pants pockets and then searched his bag while trying to steady the tiller. The keys were eventually found. Dylan meantime was almost out of sight disappearing behind a large yacht.

John and the keys went to work on the tape and the strong, thick silver staples. The box was eventually prised open, only to reveal a large plastic container with a round 'cork' in one end. John handed me the container. I couldn't prise the cork free. Muttering profanities, he went to work on the cork, which eventually surrendered to the invasive probing. Meanwhile Dylan was about ten metres away moving in ever-decreasing circles.

Battling the wind and the foamy slip-slop-slapping, the two craft attempted another reunion.

With Dylan holding our craft with one hand we managed to face away from the wind. My heart was pounding. I couldn't believe this day was going so badly. It was not how I imagined it would be. To begin the small ceremony, and close to tears, I threw the roses forward of the craft. Dylan's and my jaw dropped. The flowers were violently sucked backwards by the vortex between the two craft and floated out behind us, squashed and in a tangled mess. We watched helplessly as they floated away.

The wind was unforgiving, and in the confusion, frustration and panic, I began emptying the ashes into the water. They were never-ending and above the screaming wind, Dylan suddenly yelled, "What the devil … Mum, Connie wasn't that big!" Then the unthinkable happened. The wind changed and as I kept emptying the ashes they blew back on to us and into Dylan's eyes. He was desperately trying to hold on to our craft but now he couldn't see. "Mum, Mum", he screamed, "She's in me eye. She's in me eye! Ouch, it's stinging! Mum help!"

In the mayhem Dylan released his grip on our craft and began floating away, trying desperately to wash the stinging ash from his eyes with the salty water. Meanwhile, with tears streaming down my face, I was furiously emptying the remainder of the ashes. As Dylan slowly drifted away, John tried to manoeuvre our craft towards him. We watched aghast as the ashes, which had been dragged under the craft and churned by the small propeller, formed into a large, smoky-grey, gluggy cloud that floated out behind us. Some five metres further on the roses were drifting towards the rocky granite overhang that formed part of the shore.

We were all in shock. In mourning and frustration, I began yelling over the howling wind that I hadn't taken any photos. John managed to turn the craft around and, heading into the manic westerly we tried to catch up, only to see the ashes and the flowers were miraculously close together.

Again, this was not our day. The motor stalled and then the whole gear stick came out again, in John's hand. We were now floating without a motor or steerage while Dylan was drifting, aimlessly, still trying to wash ash from his eye.

A loud thrumming noise suddenly distracted us. Looking seaward, a ten metre launch was bearing down on us with eight people on board, playing ridiculously loud music. Had they seen us? Were they going to hit us? We sat there, rocking helplessly, with a one-eyed Dylan trying to catch us and John swearing profusely while trying to reinsert the gear stick. What seemed like an eternity, (but which probably only lasted several seconds), the launch narrowly missed us and the flowers, leaving us bobbing helplessly in its wake, like 'meerkats' on a watchful lookout. The rain abated but the wind and choppy waves were still our close companions. A red-eyed Dylan finally caught up to us and we all looked at each other, speechless – and incredulously burst out laughing. To our surprise we then saw the ashes and flowers had miraculously combined. Photos were finally taken, but we were in shock. Shocked at the misadventure of events and stunned that we were actually laughing. How badly had this day gone? We decided enough was enough and turned the craft towards the shore.

With sore red eyes and semi-blurred vision, Dylan managed to manoeuvre his craft beyond the moored yachts and headed at speed for the beach. John held our craft back allowing us a small interval, giving us the chance to take a deep breath and try to relax. Our thoughts were in turmoil.

Dylan had almost reached the shore when the craft attendant waded into the water. Dylan was trying to motor forward at full throttle and the attendant was talking to him, trying to push Dylan back out into the bay saying, "You've got heaps more time yet, go back!"

"No, no, I want to get out."

The attendant kept trying to convince Dylan to turn around when he noticed the burley.

"Hey, how come you've still got all your burley? Didn't you feed the fish? And um, what's all this black stuff all over the side of the craft?"

With a quizzical look on his face the attendant began washing the ash off. Dylan clambered out, awkwardly and reluctantly confessed our mission. The attendant just stood there, speechless.

John and I reached the beach. We climbed out into the shallows and stood there, feeling numb. As the three of us waded ashore, the sun came out, the wind died and the black clouds had all but disappeared. We were in disbelief! I stood looking at the sky, shaking my head, muttering, "Con, I can't believe what just happened."

Leaving Geordie Bay on feeble legs we ambled slowly back to the township, reliving and grappling with the day's events. On reaching the beach we noticed a ferry at the quay, and hurried to board. It was only 12.15 pm but we had had enough excitement for one day.

In hindsight I firmly believe Connie had a hand in how this day panned out. I also believe that, given the chain of events and the fact that we could see the humour, this is what Connie would have wanted. She threw down the gauntlet to test our stamina and make us laugh.

A Modern Fairy Tale

Throughout my life I have been a writer. I love it for the escape it provides and the landscapes I can travel through. A member of a writing group, we occasionally set ourselves prompts to encourage and inspire us. As you go through the rest of this memoir, I thought as writing is such a part of me, I would share some of the stories I have written. This one came from a writing group prompt that made us choose any classic fairy tale and put a 'modern' slant on it. I chose Hansel and Gretel, but of course the names have been changed to protect the not so innocent...

A fine mist hung over the mountains, which bathed the trees in a glistening glow in the early morning light. It was cool. Hannah stirred the still glowing embers in the stove and ventured outside to fill the kettle. She loved watching the mist waft its way through the valley, caressing the trees with its moist, silvery kiss. Rudy, of course, was still sound asleep.

An apocalyptic war had ravaged the land and the children now lived alone. It was a case of every man for himself. Food and amenities were scarce and the children had to survive on their wits. They had developed good survival skills, thanks to the knowledge handed down by their parents. Their father had been a woodcutter and their mother a happy homemaker, until their untimely deaths.

Although the children never knew the exact circumstances of their parents' demise, they assumed they had perished in the war. Little did they realise their father had been murdered by a jealous mountain man who lived alone, several leagues away. He had coveted the woodcutter's wife and although the children's mother had shunned his many advances, in a fit of jealous rage, the hermit murdered the woodcutter. In her grief and rage, rather than be a captive, the woman took her own life.

Hannah was twelve. A very forthright, intuitive, capable young girl, she had the hard task of caring for her younger brother. Rudy tended to be a bit dreamy, living in a world of fantasy whenever he found the time to indulge himself. Although Hannah gave in to his whims, she well knew the day would come when Rudy would have to face reality.

Hannah was handy with a bow and arrow and could easily bring down a wild bush turkey, rabbits and other small game that lived in the woods. She also managed a meagre vegetable garden with a few seasonal vegetables that would grow in the clay. The children knew of the mountain man but not what he had done. The fact that he lived several leagues away gave them no cause to come in contact with him.

This particular day Hannah decided that she and Rudy would follow a path not often used. She had an inkling deer lived in a small valley, which they had not visited for some time. She was determined to investigate.

She woke Rudy saying they needed to have breakfast, as there was some distance to travel. Rudy, in his dreamy state, wasn't in too much of a hurry, but she shooed him along, offering the temptation that she had baked some gingerbread, which was his favourite. If he was a good boy, he could have this as a reward, while on the hike.

"Can I wear your pink dress?" Rudy asked.

"My pink dress? What on earth do you want to wear that for?"

"Can I? I like the sparkles, especially when the sun shines on them and they beam pretty lights."

"No Rudy, you can't wear my pink dress. Besides, the hem is down on one side and I haven't had time to mend it."

"But I want to!"

"No."

"Then I'm not going on your silly walk."

"Fine. I'll eat the gingerbread myself."

"Nooooo!"

"Get a move on. We haven't got all day."

"No! Not unless I can wear the dress."

"Oh, for Pete's sake! Alright, but if you get it dirty you'll have to wash it."

Hannah lead the hike, carrying her bow with the quiver slung over her shoulder. She also carried a small cloth bag that held a water bottle and the gingerbread. Rudy trailed behind in the pretty pink dress. Without Hannah's knowledge, he had snatched her pink headband with the cat ears. He loved their soft texture.

Several leagues on Hannah knew she would have to leave markers for their return. The further they went, there were elements of the hike she wasn't sure of. To occupy the dreamy Rudy who was skipping along behind and humming his favourite tune, she had him place small twigs in the shape of arrows every ten trees, to mark their return.

They eventually found the valley, which was the shape of a large, elongated basin, cradled by steep, tree-covered slopes. Hannah staked out a hide to observe any grazing animals while Rudy hungrily munched on some gingerbread.

With a hand signal to be quiet, Hannah took an arrow from the quiver and carefully took steady aim. A young buck had strayed to the edge of the wood and was intent on quietly picking the fresh, juicy shoots of grass. Whoosh! The arrow was loosed and struck its deadly blow. Hannah jumped up out of the hide and ran to make sure the animal was dead and not suffering.

"C'mon Rudy. You'll have to help me." Grumbling, Rudy got to his feet and together they contrived a small sled to drag the buck back home.

The return journey proved quite a trial as the buck was heavy and the small arrows that Rudy had placed by the trees were missing. Hannah was angry that Rudy had been lax but she had enough forest knowledge and sense of direction to eventually get their tired bodies home. Hanging the buck in the small lean-to beside the house, she began the gutting process. Once done, the animal was draped in an old sheet to hang and set for the night.

Exhausted, they went inside. Hannah prepared dinner while Rudy lit the lamps and stirred the fire into life. Tired, they were quietly eating their meal when a sharp knock rapped on the door. They looked at each other with surprise and trepidation as they knew of no-one else that lived close by. Their collective antennae were on full alert. Cautiously, they moved to the stable door. The top half could be opened while the lower half remained closed. And locked. Hannah cautioned Rudy to open only the top portion, while she hid behind the door, bow and arrow at the ready.

Rudy opened the door and stood there, speechless. A large ugly man with a face resembling an elephant seal stood there. He was wearing an open leather vest that exposed his hairy chest, and his large, muscled arms were covered in tattoos. His head was shaved except for a straggly Mohawk and a solid gold earring dangled from his right ear. He was carrying an axe.

"Where's the girl?" He snarled.

"Www-hat girl?"

"Don't www-hat girl me Laddy. Where's the girl?"

Rudy gagged but had the good sense not to look to Hannah for help.

Another snarl erupted. "Ya took one 'o me deer!"

"What?"

"Listen ya little brat, I want the girl – and I want her NOW!"

Hannah had heard enough. With the bow charged, Hannah stepped around the door, took quick aim and loosed the arrow. It struck its mark right through the intruder's throat. He was dead before he hit the ground.

A Mother's Love

I am somewhat embarrassed to write this story and my son
Dylan will cringe if he ever reads it. On reflection, it is both
empathetic, pathetic and funny, and shows how your children can
stress you to the max and what lengths some of us take to try and
keep them safe.

Dylan was living with me at my unit in Osborne Park. He had
completed a course in Hospitality Management and was working
as a waiter at the Sebel Hotel in Perth. He was in his twenties, so
well on the way to being independent and very much his own
person. However, we did have one unwritten rule. If he was
intending to stay out with friends after work he would let me
know.

This worked well for both of us – he lived his life and I lived
mine. However, there was one occasion when the information
about a late night out was missed.

I went to bed at my usual hour without a worry in the world.
At some point I woke, and fairly sure I hadn't heard him return
home, I put the light on to check the time. It was around 1.00 am.
Curious, I went to check his bedroom. There was no Dylan.

Not being too concerned I put the light out and attempted to
go back to sleep. This particular night was one of those where, no
matter how hard I tried, sleep evaded me. I tossed and turned in
mounting agitation. Where was Dylan?

Rechecking the clock it was now 3.00 am and alarm bells began ringing in my head. Had I missed the staying-behind-after-work-info? I didn't think so. Had I missed the knock off time? No. He always finished at midnight. So where was he? Had something untoward happened to him? At around this time in Perth, there had been a lot of late-night problems at the Perth railway station, which is where Dylan would catch the train. Had he been mugged?

Now, I am the daughter of a policeman and the sister of an Assistant Commissioner of Police (in Victoria). I've grown up with all the fear and the bad, nasty, horrible things that can happen to innocents, and this now came into play. You also have to take into account that my dad (God rest his soul) was manic about my safety to the point of near insanity. In this instance, it had rubbed off!

I dressed and bowled out the door jumping into my car. I drove out the driveway like a speedway driver on ice. I whipped down to Scarborough Beach Road, turning right with the tyres almost smoking as I raced towards Glendalough Station. As I drew closer to the station, I slowed, zigzagging the car with my headlights shining onto the footpaths, fearing I might see a body slumped in the gutter. Fortunately, at this hour there was no traffic and, winding down the window I began calling, "D-y-l-a-n, D-y-l-a-n", at the top of my voice. Darkness and silence was all that returned. Where could he be? My distress was palpable. I broke many road rules in my agitation and despair. Driving home at a slower pace I scanned every footpath and every gutter to no avail. Reaching home my angst got the better of me. I called the police. Had there been any noticeable accidents? Had there been any muggings around the train station? Details were taken and of course I had to advise why I made the call and why I was worried. How old was my son? "He's twenty-five." There was dead silence at the end of the line, and then I could hear stifled giggling. The officer who was dealing with me was barely able to contain himself, as were the others on duty. However, he was incredibly polite and tactful as he felt he was sure that my son was ok and that Dylan had probably gone out with friends. I should go back to bed and relax.

I hung up, feeling like a complete dick! However, a mother's love just doesn't switch off that easily. I did return to bed and cried my eyes out. I was worried sick but had nowhere to go.

At 5.00 am I heard a key in the lock. Clutching a tissue to my running nose, I raced to the front door. The alcoholic vapour that wafted in almost knocked me over but the sight of seeing my son safe and sound, staggering through the door, overwhelmed me.

In a bloodshot stupor, Dylan tried desperately to focus, asking why was I up and what was wrong? The scenario that unfolded was not a pleasant one. He desperately tried to grasp the enormity of what I had done while belching through chronic alcoholic vapour. Wobbling off to his room, he collapsed onto the bed and was instantly asleep.

For the next twenty-four hours he was not a well boy and I was a mother in shame, paying for her sins. Dylan didn't speak to me for several days and even now, twenty something years later, he refuses to revisit that night!

Alexandra Bridge

I love camping and the older I become, the more I enjoy it. There is something about camping outdoors that takes you right back to basics. When I say camping, I mean camping in a tent. None of this Winnebago stuff where everything is laid on in sumptuous luxury. Not that I don't like some luxury, but camping, *real* camping, needs to be the 'rough and ready' stuff, doing it like it should be done, boiling billies and squatting around smoky fires cooking eggs and bacon, toasting bread or melting marshmallows and dribbling them over thick slices of Granny Smith apple.

So what if you've had to sleep in your clothes and still wear them the next day! All sorts of scenarios develop where this might be a probability, but is one of those processes where it strengthens character, toughens your reserve and makes you thankful for all the little luxuries you actually do have.

My friend and I decided to go away for a long weekend to Nannup, in the glorious south-west of Western Australia. Nannup is one of those small country towns that oozes hospitality, community awareness and old-world charm. Nestled in among rolling hills the town's nearest neighbours are Donnybrook, Balingup and beautiful Bridgetown, or 'Fridgetown' as the locals call it, which can be bone-chillingly cold in winter. Nannup is also home to fascinating curio shops and is one of those towns where you feel you have stepped back in time. We had been there and camped on a number of occasions and enjoyed it as a good weekend escape.

This particular day we headed for Bridgetown. The road between Bridgetown and Nannup winds through gently rolling hills with the Blackwood River snaking slowly through the sometimes steep valleys, edged by thick, eucalypt timber and lush-grassed paddocks. On cool mornings the mist wafts lazily through the gums, engulfing them in places, shrouding them from view with its moist, ghost-like cloak.

Our trip was purely for relaxation and to get away from the city humdrum. We left my workplace in the early afternoon to try and clear the city before peak period. Although the weather was cool and damp the milky-weak sunlight made the day better for its presence. We headed south, intent on camping at Alexandra Bridge, which crosses the Blackwood River on the Brockman Highway in the Shire of Augusta-Margaret River. This was one camping spot that we had visited and admired some years before and it was on our domestic bucket list of 'must do's'.

The campsite is a pretty spot on the northern side of the bridge and having crossed it, you turn right into the camp park where there are multiple choices for sites. We chose one close to the river, well in from the road. Because we arrived at around 6.00 pm, this meant erecting the tent by the headlights of the car. It was our first priority as the night chill nipped at our ears and fingers, and kept us moving to keep warm. It was vital to have the tent up so that as soon as we finished our meal we could escape the damp. It's always tricky trying to unpack and set up in the dark. We initially couldn't find the torch and kept falling over each other in our attempts to bring order out of chaos. We erected the tent away from the picnic table, which was handy to the vicinity. Once done, we heated some pre-cooked spaghetti bolognaise and settled down on to the damp, cold picnic seat with a good glass of red. We were both tired and looking forward to climbing into our sleeping bags and rugging up for the night. My car was parked alongside the picnic table facing the tent, and between the tent and the access track, giving us some small amount of privacy should anyone venture into the campground. Having had a quick read of our books to settle ourselves and give our stomachs time to digest the meal, it was lights out. Snuggling into the sleeping bags with a light but warm blanket as covering, we were soon out 'cold'.

Later, at an indeterminate time, a vehicle could be heard approaching and although it had marginally disturbed us, our depth of sleep inhibited us from waking to full consciousness. However, it only took a couple of minutes to have us wide awake with our 'antennae' fully operational. The vehicle stopped behind my car. Headlights on high beam flicked up and down across the dark expanse, illuminating the tent past the shadow of my car. Not a sound could be heard! Flick up. Silence. Flick down. Silence. Flick up. Silence. Flick down. Silence. There were no voices, no loud music, just this insidious flicking of lights. High beam, low beam, high beam, low beam, in the black nothingness of the night. We lay there motionless, barely breathing, whispering, wondering what on earth was going on. Leaden fear began to grip my gut and seep down through my legs.

We decided not to react as the sinister flicking of lights continued. Breathing shallowly, we were too intimidated to move, waiting to see what would happen next. Time appeared to stand still as we huddled in the deadly quiet. The driver suddenly began gunning the engine with the revs increasing to screaming pitch. The vehicle began to move and I was terrified it was going to smash into my car. Their vehicle was spinning round and around in a wild vortex, spraying my car with the soft, pudgy mud which covered the ground in the clearing. Around and around it went, with the engine straining against the pressure of the accelerator, the brake and the wild spinning of the wheels. Because of my car's position, this shielded the tent from the worst of the splatter, although we could hear mud hitting the flimsy fly. This scenario lasted for a couple of minutes before the vehicle stopped momentarily, then slowly turned and drove away. We could hear it disappearing down the track as waves of relief washed over us. We both sat up talking at the same time, wondering what the hell it was all about. After chewing over the event, my friend decided to get dressed in case the vehicle returned.

Unbridled fear gripped me and sent my body into convulsions of uncontrollable shaking. I shook so badly my whole body was mobile, all the time stuttering that no way was he to leave the tent. Tears coursed down my face as the fear took control. To try and ease my angst my friend pushed me down onto the pillow and, straddling my body, he sat on me with his hands pressing my shoulders into the mattress, forcing my body to wilt under the pressure. I cried and cried, begging him not to leave the tent. What if he confronted the driver and that person had a gun? What would happen if that person attacked him? What would happen to me if my friend was shot or knocked unconscious? The 'what-ifs' spilled out in a babbling torrent, exacerbating my shaking. My friend did his best to calm me down but insisted on getting dressed. Just in case! We checked our watches. It was 3.00 am.

He crawled back into his sleeping bag as I slid down into mine. The softness and warmth of familiar comfort enabled us to relax just a little, however sleep eluded us both. We lay there discussing why someone would want to do such a thing – and seemingly a lone person at that. If the vehicle had been full of Friday night revellers who had had too much to drink and were out for a bit of mischief, it would maybe have been understandable, but this event was sinister. It unravelled us.

Approximately an hour passed before we began to settle, but just as we thought we could finally close our eyes, we heard the vehicle return. I was rigid with fear, my mind in turmoil with rabid thoughts of what might happen. We lay there in the cloaked stillness of the tent, immobile, ears straining. But something didn't sound quite right. The vehicle was crashing through undergrowth some distance away, as though it was driving over logs and pushing down vegetation. Given the density of the bush, that feat would have been a challenge even in a large vehicle, which we were pretty sure it was, such as a Toyota or Nissan.

My friend extracted himself from the sleeping bag with my plaintive pleas falling on deaf ears. He armed himself with the torch and said he was going to exit the tent, but stay in its shadow until the vehicle returned. As he was about to crawl outside, the vehicle stopped. A heavy 'thump' sounded as though something solid had been hit. Maybe the vehicle had fallen into a ditch and was stuck. Shallow breathing and ears straining, we both waited in the still, silent blackness. The engine revved, then revved again. Fortunately it was still some distance away. We waited, but the dense darkness seemed to have swallowed up both vehicle and driver. After several minutes with no sounds, my friend climbed back into his sleeping bag, fully clothed and we both lay there, listening intently.

Misty daylight dawned and as we had both had a fairly tumultuous night we didn't stir until 7.30 am, glad of the sleep we did manage to have and thankful for the cold comfort of daylight. The two-man tent was small. Trying to dress sitting down is never easy. I reached for my jeans but couldn't find them. Kneeling, I rummaged through my bag, knowing I had laid my jeans on top of everything. Where were they? Asking my friend if he had seen my jeans the answer was 'no', but as he looked through his belongings he held up his jeans and looked down at his legs. In the heat of the night he had mistakenly grabbed my jeans and put them on. Given the events of the night this allowed us to relax and have a good laugh.

The morning was bone cold and damp, with thick fog blanketing the river. Anaemic sunlight desperately tried to make an impression through the mist. We surveyed the site. The back of my car was coated with mud. We were amazed at how much mud had actually landed on the tent, which looked like it had large brown polka dots all over one side. The damage the spinning vehicle had done to the turf showed the extent of the velocity that was used. A huge circle had been gouged out of the wet ground. Although the car and tent were a mess, we were grateful there was no other damage.

Initially we had intended to spend the whole weekend at this site but after the events of the night neither of us wanted to be anywhere near the place. Over breakfast we decided to decamp and seek a more congenial site. Having packed everything away, it was now teeth brushing time. My friend wandered off in the direction of some trees on the other side of the track and I walked some little distance away from where the tent had been, on the edge of the bush and close to the river bank. I was busily brushing my *pearly whites* while facing into the mist-cloaked bush when I turned – and stopped dead in midbrush.

There was an elongated piece of granite, just over knee-high, standing at a slight angle among the bracken and untidy dry grass. It looked incongruous and totally out of place as there were no other rocks around. A lone sentinel on a silent watch. As it was facing away from the camp I stepped around the rock only to discover a plaque on its face. With the toothbrush stuck sideways in my mouth, I was curious to see the inscription. A multitude of emotions bombarded my senses. I was rooted to the spot. I didn't know whether to cry or to run. The plaque was a memorial to a young man who had committed suicide at this very spot only a few years before. My ability to comprehend the implications of what happened the night before, deserted me. I stood there completely stunned. Was last night's event linked to this tragic spot? Was the person in the vehicle a relative of the deceased? Were they angry that someone was camped so close? Had this happened to other people who may have camped here? Question after question crowded my brain without any answers swimming through the cataract of fog that engulfed my thoughts.

I called out to my friend in a choking whimper, "You better come here."

"Why, what's the matter?"

"Just come here. You need to see this."

***

A subdued pair, we left that campsite with emotions running hot. Not knowing where to camp but wanting to be as far away from everyone and everything, we scoured the area until we settled on a high, tree-covered ridge in a seriously isolated spot. I doubt we could ever find that place again. I was concerned at the time that we would never find our way out, we were so *buried* in the bush. On selecting the site, my friend dragged two huge logs onto the track above our camp, effectively sandwiching the site between the logs. If anyone did come along they would not be able to pass.

We spent Saturday exploring the bush and enjoying the freedom of the wide-open spaces, but our thoughts and conversation constantly returned to the previous twenty-four hours.

Although we love Nannup, it was a long time before we returned to camp there again.

Contact From The Other Side

Several years after Connie passed away I visited a friend in New South Wales while also wanting to make contact with a friend of hers. Connie owned an oyster farm at Narooma and she bequeathed the farm to Jack when she died. She was very fond of him and very grateful when earlier he had taken over management of the farm. While he did the majority of the physical work, Connie kept the books and paid the bills. Narooma is a picturesque seaside town on the south coast of New South Wales. Its name is Aboriginal, meaning 'clear blue waters'.

Connie had been so excited at the time of the purchase. Her enthusiasm had rubbed off. Hence my interest to see what had her captivated prior to her illness. Contacting Jack hadn't been easy and I had the feeling he wasn't too keen on me visiting.

My friend and I found our way to Jack's and knocked at the door. It was a typical seaside shack that had obviously been built many years previously. It was painted pale blue, and through the louvres, thin curtains swayed in the gentle breeze. Music was coming from a back room and for several moments, I thought we either hadn't been heard or no-one was home. At last footsteps approached and a very tall, tanned, muscular man with a moustache and short, balding grey hair opened the wire door. It never fails to surprise me that no matter how you imagine someone, they never look how you picture them. Jack was quietly spoken and if anything a bit shy, but he invited us in and offered to make a cup of tea.

While the pot was brewing we exchanged interesting and happy stories about Connie. Jack said how surprised and grateful he was that she had been generous enough to leave him the farm. He looked as though he had had a pretty tough life. That certainly came across without him divulging too much. I was personally pleased that the farm had been left in such good and capable hands.

Even though the chat was friendly, there seemed to be a hesitancy about Jack, which I couldn't fathom, until he said he had something for me, from Connie. I was a little taken aback. Connie had left me money in her will but I certainly wasn't expecting to receive anything else.

Jack disappeared into the back room and returned with a photo frame. The enclosed photo was of Connie and Jack and all the people who either worked for her or owned oyster farms themselves. The photo was unusual in that Connie was the only female in the group, although this didn't surprise me. Jack then explained that after he had received my initial letter making contact, and my phone call to him, he was in the back room that serves as his office when suddenly, out of the blue, the photo frame went flying across the room and landed on the cement floor several feet away. The glass shattered and the photo became dislodged. Jack went on to explain that there was no wind that day and he certainly hadn't knocked the frame because he wasn't close enough.

On picking up the broken pieces he noticed something tucked in behind the photo and the backing. He handed me a card, which I instantly recognised. It was the last card I sent Connie before she passed, telling her how much I cared for her and how much I would miss her. Many tears spilled. Jack reiterated that he wasn't

into the paranormal, but he realised that Connie knew I would be
visiting and she wanted me to have the card.

Croatia

Seeping quiet. I looked about me – the only tourist in the spacious hotel lobby. Although the reception staff occupied their desks, you could have heard a pin drop. Stepping outside into the cool morning air, nothing moved. Not another soul was in sight. The silence was unusual for a large city.

Looking around to establish some bearings and local landmarks, I traversed a pockmarked road criss-crossed by tramlines. The surrounding buildings were old but beautiful in an aged way. The architecture was regal although the outer surfaces were dilapidated. The buildings stood proud in their albeit shabby, three and four stories, yet held their age with a certain quiet pride. Because of soft cloud cover and the black asphalt damp with dew, the street seemed to swallow the early light. I passed huge splintered, weathered, wooden double doors on each building, the handles and metal locks all differed in design. Some of the more elegant buildings were painted in soft yellows and creams. These stood out from the older drab greys which were shedding their outer cement layer, uncovering ancient, handmade chipped bricks beneath. Against the lighter coloured structures that looked fresh and ready to meet the new day, the older tenements exuded superficial tiredness, as if resigned to their fate.

Turning into a beautiful tree-lined avenue, a sumptuous park ran through its middle. The trees were in full leaf and a large fountain ahead was spraying misty rainbows in the weak dappled sunlight. People were beginning to stir.

Faint music could be heard. I increased my pace. There was activity ahead. Before me was a vast open square bordered by tramlines and backed by tall city buildings. A massive statue in the centre of the square was of an older man in full battle regalia. Wearing armour, he was wielding a large sword and sitting astride a magnificent galloping horse.

A piano accordion, guitars and a violin were playing from behind many small gazebo-type tents, which sat in tidy lines behind the statue. This was a Saturday morning market. Suddenly, colourful costume-clad dancers stepped out, clapping, singing and dancing, accompanied by the small band. The bright reds, whites and yellows of the dancers' clothes vibrated as they danced, catching my attention and the verve and joy they showed was intoxicating. Everyone had a smile on their face. A large crowd formed and some of the dancers pulled clapping onlookers into their rhythmic performance. Young children in similar colourful costumes helped make up the dance numbers. They were obviously being trained by their elders in the old customs.

This was Zagreb – Croatia at its best!

***

For the next ten days, I joined *Insight's Country Roads of Croatia* tour visiting Slovenia, Opatija, Pula, Revinij, Split, Plitvice National Park, Hvar, Korcula, Dubrovnik and Montenegro, in addition to several other towns and villages in between.

Four of the scariest things when you travel, particularly when you're a single, older woman, are if you lose your passport; you don't have any money; you miss your flight and you don't speak the language. On this trip I managed three of the above.

Once the tour concluded, I flew from Dubrovnik to Zagreb to catch my return flight home to Perth. Suffice to say I confused the departure time and missed the flight. I didn't hear my name being called until the very last moment and, running like the wind, I arrived at the gate just as they closed it. They wouldn't let me through.

Anyone who has ever been caught in a situation like this knows the gut-wrenching feeling. The ground staff were furious. My pleading fell on deaf ears. I knew instantly where I made the error and had no-one to blame but myself. Naturally I was upset but my inner self told me to learn from the mistake. Don't panic. Find the positive. Things happen for a reason. I decided to look at it as an adventurous misadventure.

My text home read, 'I have missed my flight. This is not a joke!'

Igor, the young man responsible for looking after people like myself, took me under his wing and booked a new flight. My biggest dilemma was I had almost no Croatian money left. How was I going to pay for a hotel and buy something to eat? I had no foreign currency to change.

Igor checked with the taxi drivers outside regarding the fare to a hotel. I couldn't cover the fare. Igor advised the charge was outrageous anyway. He had a plan! He made phone calls to several accommodation venues close to the airport and finally secured a room. Yes, they would accept a credit card. He then offered to drive me to the accommodation on his way home, however I would have to wait until he signed off work, one and a half hours later.

From a side street, Igor pointed out the building. I thanked him profusely as he had also booked a taxi for the following morning, for the return to the airport.

Dragging my suitcase across ancient, rough cobbled stones to the 'blue light' Igor had indicated, I had to smile. The accommodation was so old I reckon it had been built before Jesus was born. The room was basic, however the bed was comfortable and the plumbing worked. I was very grateful! Beggars can't be choosers.

It was 9.00 pm. The receptionist indicated the direction of some restaurants. With the night closing in and my heart in my mouth I walked the near deserted, darkening streets in some trepidation. My *aloneness* engulfed me. The chosen restaurant fortunately looked clean and presentable and the omelette I ordered was one of the best I've ever eaten. The meal cost A$3.00. As communication was near impossible, they accepted the credit card when I waved it. This helped to buoy up my emotions.

At breakfast the following morning I managed to gather some bread, meat, cheese, a boiled egg and some fruit and smuggled it out in a large serviette, for lunch. The taxi arrived and my meagre Croatian funds just managed to cover the fare. Sitting next to the departure gate as though glued to it, I was first in line at the boarding call. With a ten-hour stopover at Doha, I arrived home two days after I was due.

Two weeks later an email arrived from Igor. He was checking I had arrived home safely.

The Bridesmaid

In 2014, having recently self-published my memoir, *Two Shakes of a Dead Lamb's Tail,* I attended the Easter Show at Beverley, in the wheatbelt. To decorate the new gazebo I had lots of photos of Bougainville and the sheep station pinned to cork boards, to attract customers. Around morning teatime a middle-aged couple wandered past and took an interest in the book and the photos. The wife eventually wandered off but the gentleman remained enthralled. Having read the back cover he began asking questions and advised that he and his wife had also lived in New Guinea, in the highlands. They lived there for seventeen years and their four children were born there.

It's always interesting to swap stories about life in PNG, particularly as we both lived there pre-independence. The conversation continued, and I asked the gentleman where did he live now? He explained they hailed from Heyfield in Victoria but were currently in WA looking after their daughter as she was ill.

"Oh", I said, "I have a girlfriend who lives in Heyfield, but I doubt you would know her."

The gentleman responded saying, "Heyfield isn't exactly a huge place. What's her name?"

"Rosemary Dunworth."

The man stared at me for a few moments. "Rosemary is my wife's best friend and she was our bridesmaid."

Goosebumps shot up my arms and I stood there, mouth open, catching flies.

We had lots more to talk about. I told him I was named after Rosemary's mum as my mum really liked the name *Noreen*. She felt it was different. Rosemary and I grew up together in Ross Street, Surrey Hills in Melbourne. We also went to school together, although Rosemary was a year ahead of me.

Eventually his wife returned to my site. "Well", I said, "you've just missed out on the story of the century." She smiled and looked quizzically at her husband. He just grinned and said to me, "You tell her!"

Like me, she was gobsmacked. Apparently Rosemary and Tamara had shared a flat while they were both at Teachers' College and had travelled overseas together.

I couldn't wait to get home and ring Rosemary.

"Hey Ro, guess what?"

"I dunno. What?"

"Guess who I just met while at a market in the wheatbelt?"

"Oh I dunno. Who?"

"Alec and Tamara."

"GET OUTTA HERE!"

Home Invasion

In 2004 Andrew's wife travelled to Christmas Island as part of her job. This meant Andrew would be home with Liam, nine and Emily five. To give him some support I drove to Australind to spend a weekend to help out. Dylan was contemplating coming also, but as his uni exams were looming he chose to stay home.

I never like sleeping with a closed bedroom door and through the night I was suddenly aware of indeterminate noise, and the kitchen light was on. Having come out of a deep sleep, I lay there trying to decipher what was happening. Donning my dressing gown as the night was quite cool, I stepped out past the dividing wall, only to discover Andrew wasn't in the kitchen and all the outside lights were on. This had me puzzled. I went over to the laundry door, which led into the carport. Peering outside, I saw Andrew dressed in his pyjamas and dressing gown. He was standing in the backyard near the large sliding door that was entry to the family room, talking to a tall, solid man who was around thirty years of age. This person was dressed in a sports jacket and pants and wasn't someone I recognised.

Andrew kept asking the bloke, "What are you doing and why are you in my backyard?" No answers were forthcoming and in between Andrew pressing the man for an answer, I asked him what was going on.

"It's ok Mum, go back to bed."

"But what's going on? Who is this guy?"

"Mum, go back to bed. I'll deal with this."

Hesitation; confusion; niggling fear, instinct told me to stand my ground.

"I think I'll just stay here for a bit."

"Why are you in my backyard? Answer me. I want to know why you are in my backyard and why were you licking my back door? It's 1.00 am. Why are you here? I don't know who you are but I want you to leave and I want you to leave now."

The man, who had indeed been licking the door, slowly exited the backyard gate, mumbling incoherently. He began to walk between the two cars parked in the carport. I was standing guard by the laundry door ready to slam it shut in case he attempted to come inside. My emotions were running amok because I was afraid for Andrew and fearful this bloke might try and force his way into the house.

Because his speech was incoherent, and the whole situation was extremely suspicious, I said in a very loud voice, "I'm going to ring the police."

"Oh, that's ok. You do that" the bloke replied, with a stupid half-smile on his face and eyes that indicated his brain was in another sphere. Shutting the laundry door, I fled to the phone, dialled 000, requested the police and explained we had an unidentified person at Andrew's address and could someone please attend. I was told that they were very sorry but they had their hands full chasing several wanted people through the local swamp. There was no available backup. I was in disbelief.

Being concerned for the kids I ventured into Liam's room, only to find him wide awake. Naturally he wanted to know what was going on. So as not to alarm him I told him that someone was in the backyard and that his dad was trying to get them to leave. Liam was understandably distressed. After allaying his fears as best I could, I told him that under no circumstances was he to get out of bed. I reassured him that I would not be far away, but he must stay put.

Returning to the laundry I tentatively opened the door. The bloke was still standing in the carport, talking gibberish, with Andrew still attempting to move him on. I said I'd phoned the police and of course he wanted to know if they were on their way. Not wanting to alert the bloke that no help was forthcoming, I said in a booming but quavering voice, "yes, they'll be here soon", but signalled Andrew this was not the case.

The bloke turned away looking like he intended to leave. Without warning he turned suddenly and grabbed Andrew in a headlock and began punching him in the face. I screamed, slammed the laundry door and ran, hitting this guy over the head with my hands. Andrew was powerless as he was in a fast hold. The bloke was just punching, punching, punching. Blood began streaming down Andrew's white, distraught face as I was frantically trying to pull the bloke off him, screaming all the time, "get off him, get off him you fucking bastard!"

Unfortunately for Andrew and myself I had no weapon to hit this bloke with. The whole time I was smacking and punching him, my mind was racing as to what I could lay my hands on to make him let Andrew go. If I ever had that time over again I know exactly what I should have done.

As fast as the attack happened, he suddenly let Andrew go. Andrew staggered to one side, trying to gain equilibrium. I raced inside to grab a towel or anything I could find to wipe his face. In the process I rang the police again, screaming down the phone that my son had been attacked, demanding immediate assistance be made available. I then raced in to check on the kids. Liam was close to tears but I hugged him tight and told him under no circumstances was he to come outside. Emily, fortunately, was sound asleep.

Returning to the carport, the intruder was still standing between the cars. Andrew's pyjamas had been shredded in the subsequent struggle and he was standing there, bleeding, but holding his own. He looked like a tattered scarecrow. As I stepped outside another man was standing against the wall just near the laundry door. I looked up in astonishment as I hadn't seen him before. Panic surged through me because I thought he was with the attacker.

"Who the hell are you?"

"It's ok, I'm the neighbour from next door. My wife and I have been lying in bed listening to the screaming and I thought I'd better come and see if I could lend a hand."

I didn't know whether to hug him or kick him. I was so distraught I couldn't understand why half the street hadn't turned out to help because I'm sure the racket would have woken more than one household.

The intruder suddenly began to walk, quite quickly, towards the street. It was almost as if he had 'woken up' and come to the realisation that he better move himself. Walking briskly, Andrew began to follow him with the neighbour hot on both their heels. All three vanished into the night. Overcome with fear and emotion I went back into the house, locked the laundry door and stood watch by the kitchen window for Andrew's return. Approximately twenty minutes passed when I heard a vehicle, and on venturing out, the police had arrived. Andrew was talking to them.

As it turned out, the intruder disappeared into a neighbour's house on the other side of the laneway that ran between the two houses. When the police questioned the occupants of that household, all knowledge of the event was denied, even though the attacker was one of those questioned.

Andrew eventually returned inside looking more like his old self, but with a badly bruised, swollen and bloodied face. He went off to have a shower while I put the kettle on and went to reassure Liam. Without divulging that Andrew had been bashed, I consoled Liam enough to settle him down with a big hug and a kiss and told him to go back to sleep. His dad was ok. He was having a shower and we were going to have a cup of tea.

Over the cuppa, Andrew and I talked the events through. As a mother, all I wanted to do was protect my 'baby' and look after him. My kids have always been hardy types and Andrew was having none of it. He was 'ok' in his estimation, which made me feel helpless. But what could I do? I retired, with Andrew reassuring me he was ok and it was time we both got some sleep. However, the kitchen light stayed on for a long time while Andrew no doubt, relived the night.

Morning dawned and a very subdued household eventually rose to meet the day. Liam and I were both keeping a watchful eye on Andy whereas Emily, who fortunately had slept through the whole debacle, was totally oblivious of the midnight carnage.

The right-hand side of Andrew's face was severely swollen and his right eye was bloodshot and sore. After breakfast, we went outside so I could take photos of his face and then *insisted* that he see a doctor, which he agreed to.

We managed to get through the rest of Sunday. I had hung around, partly because I was loath to leave and partly because the police were supposed to come to interview us both. At 2.00 pm I could wait no longer. I had to return to Perth for work the next day. I phoned Dylan to let him know I was leaving and would be home a bit later than expected. I also told him, briefly, about the attack. He was shattered and wanted to know more, but I said I would fill him in once I was home.

All the way home I relived the previous night's event and the shock began to set in. I don't remember most of that trip because my emotions were in overdrive. What could I have done better? Why couldn't I have helped Andrew more? Different scenarios played themselves out, over and over again. I was crying and in huge emotional pain. The disbelief that the assault had happened was still ripe and Andrew's ghostly, bloodied face was indelibly etched in my psyche.

As I pulled into the car park at home, Dylan raced out the door and grabbed me, a thousand questions pouring from him, his emotion palpable. It was then I let go. I cried and cried and cried, all the while trying to disgorge the details and becoming hopelessly entangled in the facts. Although it was understandable, Dylan became so angry – angry that it had happened to his brother – angry that he wasn't there to help. It was another highly emotive night.

The following morning as I was getting ready for work, my knees buckled. I rang my HR Manager and explained. She managed to book me into the Company's Assistance Program for a 9.00 am appointment and I have to say it was my saving grace. The counsellor was so helpful and supportive. I explained how every time I closed my eyes, Andrew's bloodied face would swim before me. She told me that many people who have a similar experience describe the same sort of scenario. I also told her how helpless I felt and that I hadn't done enough to help him. My list went on and on. Within that support, she told me that it was very important that I tell Andrew how helpless I felt, that I hadn't done enough to assist him, and how that made me feel.

Dylan, on the other hand, remained angry and hostile. He barely spoke for three days. This was another concern as it didn't matter what I tried, I couldn't placate him. It wasn't his fault that he wasn't there but his seeming guilt and anger rode him like a fiery demon.

I did ring Andrew a few days after my counselling appointment and we had a chat. Andrew said he was just so pleased I was there as he was worried for the kids' sake. If I hadn't been there he wasn't quite sure what he would have done. I understood, but I still felt I hadn't done enough while he was being attacked. Resilience is an amazing tool. Andrew, out of the whole family, was the most calm about the whole episode, whereas Dylan and I were wound tighter than clockwork springs.

My experience with traumatic occurrences is that the hardest 'hit' often overwhelms the people on the sidelines, whereas the 'victim' is sometimes the one who seems to ride out the trauma best.

The intruder was identified and charged with assault. A court case was held and because it was his first offence, he was given a twelve-month good behaviour bond. During the hearing he apparently apologised to the family for the distress he had caused.

Finding Jeanie

Finding Jeanie is a result of the Creative Writing Course I did at the beginning of 2019. We had to create a character with low self-esteem who aspired to something better; Jeanie is who popped out of my head.

Jeanie Miller sat at the nurses' station cautiously observing who was around while wringing her hands in agitation. Her head was spinning. The senior nurse position had just been advertised at the Aged Care Facility where she worked and Jeanie was seriously interested. Her mother had been the senior nurse years ago and had an empathetic and caring personality. Everyone admired her and now she was one of the residents.

The 'what-ifs' crowded Jeanie's brain. She needed to get a grip. Why had this been posted now?

There was so much to do this morning. Clients needed washing; medications had to be dispensed; Mrs Weisingham needed an enema and last night's dinner dishes were still sitting on Mr Blake's table tray. All Jeanie wanted to do was go somewhere quiet so she could wrap her head around the application. She had to get this job. She just 'had' to!

Jeanie donned her protective clothing and attended Mrs Weisingham. These jobs were never pleasant but it had to be done. The elderly lady had several medical issues and was always pleased when Jeanie was the attending nurse.

"You're so good to me," Mrs Weisingham wheezed, as Jeanie gently turned the old lady on to her side and began the procedure. "I know this is a very unpleasant job for you girls, but I'm always glad when it's you on duty."

Jeanie smiled. "It's ok Mrs Weisingham. Us girls are used to this. We do this sort of thing nearly every day. It's part of our job."

"I know dear, but I really appreciate everything you do for me. You really are my favourite nurse."

"Thank you Mrs Weisingham. I sincerely appreciate your comments."

***

Jeanie returned to the nurses' station. Several of the younger staff were checking out the daily roster and liaising with Jeanie regarding who to attend next. The day was rapidly disappearing and Jeanie's tension began to mount. Her nemesis was the Facility's Manager, Terry Kramer, a strong-minded no-nonsense woman who always made Jeanie feel insignificant. If she didn't gain this position she knew what self-esteem she had would be lost. She craved the responsibility, and to a degree, the admiration her mother had achieved. But what would the other staff think if she applied? Jeanie needed to talk to her husband. She couldn't actually wait to leave this day as the pungent disinfectant smell was overpowering. She could feel it coating her tongue.

"Nurse Miller, didn't I tell you to get those sheets taken care of two hours ago? Get onto it woman. Honestly, I don't know why I put up with you sometimes!"

Jeanie jumped, yelped in surprise then slid past Nurse Kramer, having gathered up the soiled sheets in her arms, eyes cast down so as not to offend. Frightened that maybe this time her boss might actually strike her, Jeanie wondered, not for the first time, why she put up with such abuse. Yes, it was abuse. She knew it, and so did everyone else.

"Yes, Nurse Kramer. Would you like me to take these towels as well?" Terry Kramer rolled her eyes and dismissed the grown woman with a wave of her hand as if she were a naughty child. Tears of humiliation gathered unbidden and filled Jeanie's eyes.

Terry Kramer was middle-aged and unmarried. She had risen through the nursing ranks because of her uncompromising abilities and partly because her ambition drove her. Jeanie was afraid of Terry. She was aware that although Terry rarely communicated her thoughts, Terry's body language and demeanour conveyed veiled displeasure. Jeanie often pondered if the woman used her unpleasant, abusive nature to make up for her short stature and stocky build. Was this one way Terry could throw her weight around? Jeanie inwardly cowered every time Terry appeared. She was sure Terry could read her vibes. The two women had worked with each other in various departments over many years, but their working relationship never developed beyond formal grounds. They were the total antithesis of each other.

Terry had seen Jeanie's application for the senior nursing position and entered the ward just as Jeanie was finishing with a patient. Without any salutation Terry said, "Nurse Miller, come to my office at your earliest convenience," then disappeared behind a swirl of blue curtain.

Jeanie's bowels lurched. Her nerve ends were on fire when she entered the office.

"Don't bother sitting down Nurse Miller. This will only take a moment." Jeanie blanched but held her nerve.

"I've seen your application for the senior nurse position and I have to tell you I'm not impressed. Although you are a very capable nurse I consider you don't have the 'grunt', which is the only word I can use, for this position. Senior nursing responsibilities go far beyond knowing about patient care and I have to say your personality demonstrates weakness of character. We don't need that in this position. You would have to oversee the other nursing staff, relieve me on occasions and with all the paperwork this job entails, I feel you are not up to those responsibilities."

Jeanie stood there, paralysed. She knew this wasn't going to be a barrel load of laughs but she wasn't quite prepared for this onslaught. Her bottom lip quivered, her mind and heart were racing – this was do or die. How on earth was she going to keep the quaver out of her voice?

"I'm sorry," Jeanie began, "but you're wrong." As she said this, her back straightened and she squared her shoulders. "I'm every bit as good as you are at the job. I may lack your 'grunt', as you put it, but I refuse to rescind my application." With that she turned smartly and walked out the door.

"Nurse Miller," stormed Terry, her voice ricocheting off the green corridor walls, "come back here this minute." You could have heard a pin drop.

Jeanie halted. She realised this was the step up or shut up moment. All her life she had aspired for a role like this. If she didn't fight for herself now, the chance would never come again. Something tangible rose within. Marching back into Terry's office, Jeanie slammed the door.

"How dare you speak to me like that," Jeanie yelled. "Who the hell do you think you are? Just because I'm not like you – overbearing, loud-mouthed and rude – doesn't mean I'm not capable of a senior role."

"Oh really," snarled Terry. "Little Miss People Pleaser. Trying to ingratiate yourself with everyone. It's sickening."

"The only thing that's sickening," Jeanie snapped, "is your grandiose attitude to everyone and everything. How about you grow a personality! You think I'm trying to ingratiate myself, well that's your crap opinion, but at least people 'LIKE' me, which is more than anyone can say about you!"

Terry gaped and flopped backwards into her chair. No-one had ever spoken to her like that before.

"Get out of my office NOW," Terry sneered.

***

One week later, Jeanie sat in the local park under the shade of a large jacaranda. The sunlight splashed through the fern-like leaves creating mottled shadows that danced on the grass. She ran her fingers through the grassy tufts, enjoying the soft sensation while quietly humming a random tune. She was entranced for a while with the shadow play. A gentle smile crossed her face and her eyes sparkled with moisture. She took a deep, satisfied breath. The job was hers.

It was strange, but the feeling that flowed through her body was both gratifying and uplifting. Jeanie had found her voice. She knew what she was capable of. Her voice was here to stay. Never again would she allow herself to be cowed by anyone, and basking in the small amount of glory she allowed herself, she turned her face to the sun.

Hot Cross Vicar

Tungamah is a small country town in north-eastern Victoria and is where my husband grew up on a sheep/wheat property. A close-knit, small farming community, everyone attended church on Christmas morning and woe-betide if anyone was missing. My mother-in-law lived next door to the Anglican Church and always 'busied' herself on Easter Sunday, hurrying everyone along to be ready for church on time. Our son, Andrew, was eighteen-months old and quite a handful. Sitting still and being quiet was not his forte and I was silently dreading the service.

We entered the church and to my chagrin my mother-in-law insisted on sitting three rows from the front. I had been hoping for a back seat and a quick escape, if necessary. The service began. Andrew was all eyes and ears for the first ten minutes but then the squirming started, so he was continuously passed backwards and forwards to various adult relatives to try and keep him quietly entertained.

The service progressed with Father Goldsworthy in the thick of prayers and atonements. While swinging a chalice, which held a lighted candle, it was brushing against his vestments. Suddenly they caught fire. I think I saw this before anyone else but was so shocked my voice failed me. I watched dumbstruck, as flames blackened his robe and steadily climbed past his right knee, heading north.

All hell broke loose as someone in the front pew made a wild grab for him while at the same time the Vicar started banging his robes in a fury. Self-immolation was avoided! After the shouting and gasps subsided, with the smell of burnt cloth hanging heavy in the air, Father Goldsworthy casually smiled and commented that he wasn't quite ready to meet his 'Maker'.

Swimming with Whale Sharks

Swimming with whale sharks has always been on my bucket list. However, being underwater engenders both excitement and fear for me – coupled with dread. My daughter and I departed Perth in June 2013. We spent our first night camping at Cue, the beautiful historic town on the Great Northern Highway some 700 km from Perth.

Statewide, there had been huge storms and heavy rains during this particular winter. Further north, having been soaked at Auski Roadhouse and washed out in Karijini National Park, we pulled into a 24-hour campsite midway between Parabadoo and Nanutarra. The only reasonable site left was in a dry, stony creek bed. All other comfortable, sandy campsites were occupied. We prayed the creek wouldn't flood during the night.

***

Once we reached Exmouth, because of the forecast, Mel's gut instinct told her not to delay the booking. Two days grace gave us time to relax from the long drive.

The morning of the dive was cool. Weak, golden sunlight bordered the straggly clouds as we stood shivering, waiting for the bus to collect us. I was fascinated with the two girls who checked us in. Here we were rugged up to the nines whereas these two, who were both very tanned, were wearing short shorts and sleeveless shirts. They laughed and giggled all the way to the boat, seemingly without a thought for the temperature.

A small dinghy transferred us to the cruiser. With twenty tourists aboard we headed towards the limitless horizon. There was a slight swell and wispy cloud cover. I'm not a strong swimmer and was already having misgivings. Mel, who is slightly built and thin, was really worried about the water temperature. We were supplied with half wetsuits, snorkels, fins, and goggles. A helicopter was also employed to spot the whale sharks, if any.

Twenty minutes into the trip, a pod of orcas were seen diving through the waves, ten metres off the port side of the boat. Everyone was excited, except me. Being dressed in a black wet suit, I didn't fancy being taken for a seal by a killer whale. I asked one of the crew if the orcas were likely to hang around. The answer came back, 'no'. Orcas weren't often seen, so this was a great treat! I proffered a pathetic smile. The band of fear that had tightened around my head needed to be severed but I couldn't quite find the place to begin the cut.

Facing any fear is like passing through an automatic gate. Once past, the gate closes behind you. There's no turning back and whatever the consequences, there's always another gate ahead.

Attempting to conjure up a positive note, one of Winston Churchill's quotes came to mind: "Fear is a reaction. Courage is a decision."

We soon received notice that a whale shark was heading our way and a mad scramble ensued to enter the water. At my age and not being the most agile, I hung back so as not to impede other swimmers. In we went. From my perspective there was total chaos, with a multitude of arms and legs in frenzied thrashing.

Looking down into the choppy water, this enormous leopard-spotted whale shark glided past as though in a dream. Because of their size, little is required regarding fin and tail movement and yet this fish almost vanished before my eyes, such was its momentum. It made my head swim! I couldn't keep up and to my chagrin everyone else was metres in front of me enjoying swimming along with the shark. I have to say that even though I was the tailender, the perfection of this amazing animal had me awestruck. There was a multitude of suckerfish clinging to the whale shark's body, diligently nibbling the miniscule parasites from its enormous, spotted body. Several smaller fish were lazily swimming in and out of its great gaping maw.

The excitement soon waned as the whale vanished in a deep dive, in what appeared to be a fathomless void. Everyone headed back to the boat. By this time the swell had increased, and with the choppy water, I had some difficulty in climbing aboard. Thankfully one of the crew managed to haul me onto the platform. Everyone was talking about their experience. I turned to see Mel sitting in the middle of the boat, swathed in towels, her lips blue. I panicked. Some of the crew threw blankets around her and thankfully gave her a warm drink. Several women began rubbing her back and legs, trying to stimulate some circulation.

It wasn't long before the call went out again. We all fell back into the water, with one of the crew assisting me, swimming with me and literally pulling me along so I could keep up. She was only about 157 cm but could swim like a fish and pulled me along as though I was a piece of foam rubber. Swimming with one of these spectacular animals proved very emotional. Their bulk is massive but they exude such calm, nonchalant acceptance, making the experience all the more unforgettable – spiritual.

After lunch we entered the water again to drift with the current, with the view to exploring the reef below. Although I have snorkelled on many previous occasions, this was quite magical. As above, so it is below. Mountains and valleys, boulders and rocks, plants of all descriptions, colours, shapes and sizes, clinging to pinnacles and waving gracefully with the current in a gentle rhythmic dance. Small fish abounded and reef sharks were seen sussing out nooks and crannies in among the coral. A young turtle became caught up in the mix of swimmers and swiftly dived to make its escape.

When the call came regarding a fifth whale shark, most of the swimmers again hit the water. Owing to the hour of the day, Mel chose to stay on board as the water temperature had cooled further. We climbed to the top deck and watched in awe as this enormous whale shark glided past. The size indicated it was an adult male.

We saw five whale sharks that day and were told by the crew we were lucky to have seen one!

Welcome to My Nightmare

Some Creative Writing Course exercises limit you to the amount of words you can use. In this case, only 300 words to describe someone's nightmare.

Alice Cooper's song *Welcome To My Nightmare*, was a resonating echo, the tune annoyingly persistent in Milly's head. A large, grotesque figure with long black dreadlocks approached her, bearing a livid, red-lipped lopsided grin. His eyes were circled with large black rings and his teeth were pointed like fangs. Swirling filaments of green and purple vapour accompanied his every move. Milly cringed.

"Wh-whh who are you," she stammered.

The red leer widened, baring his tar-coloured teeth.

"Why Milly," the voice sarcastically croaked, "You know who I am. You've been singing my song on and off all day."

Drool slid through the leer as a white-gloved hand reached out towards her.

"Don't you touch me," Milly squeaked, "Don't you dare!"

"Sorry my dear," the spectre croaked. "I don't mean to scare you. I just want to touch your soft, silky skin." His mouth drooped in disappointment but his eyes glistened.

"You stay away from me. Who are you? I don't know you."

"Ahh, but you do my dear. I'm never far from your thoughts. I'm the bad boy you long for in your dreams."

"N-n-nooooo you're not," Milly squealed. "I'm m-married. Why would I ever think about someone like you?"

The leer widened as a loud, mocking laugh rang out.

"Come come, my dear. This won't hurt a bit."

Milly gargled a strangled scream as something heavy landed on top of her.

"Mummy, Mummy, why did you scream? Mummy, I need to do a wee. NOW!"

Milly gasped. Her heart was pounding. Realisation surfaced as she tried to untangle her feet from the scrunched-up sheets. She scrambled from the bed, almost tripping as the sweat-drenched sheets still clung to her feet.

"Hurry Lucy. Quick! You're my second nightmare."

A Letter from
Afghanistan

This letter was written by a friend to his family. It is included here because it was written at a time when it was more common for Europeans to travel through Middle Eastern countries. It was six years prior to the Russian invasion. The group left from London with *Indigo Overland Expeditions* and travelled through France, Belgium, Germany, Austria, Yugoslavia, Greece, Turkey, Syria, Lebanon, Israel, Jordan, Iraq, Iran, Afghanistan, Pakistan, Kashmir, India and Nepal. It provides a view of the world, and more particularly Afghanistan at that time, that most of us will never see.

12th January 1973

Dear All

I am sitting in the public area of the Mayfair hotel in Kandahar, Afghanistan, having sent my last letter from Tehran.

Leaving Tehran on third January, we headed across snow-covered mountains on our way through Iran and ran into a problem. A tanker had dropped a trailer off a semi causing the tank to rupture. The contents, which can be likened to molasses, spilled down the mountain road. No-one appeared game to drive through the spillage, but after examination our coach driver, John, decided to give it a go, having offloaded us first. Three--quarters of the way through and with no more traction, a contingent of men from our coach lent a helping hand. We were away – to a round of applause from the locals, who were now game to try. We stayed that night in Gorgon.

The following day was uneventful until late in the afternoon when the coach windows began to ice up, just like the inside of a refrigerator, despite antifreeze in the heater hoses. These snapped while John worked on thawing out the system. The Bedford diesel spluttered and stopped. John assumed the diesel had frozen, as can happen. He proceeded to fill containers with oil and kerosene, one of which he lit, placing it under the fuel tank and injector pump. You cannot imagine the difficulty of trying to do this in the extreme cold. It is around -30 °C, no joke. Some of us helped John fill the containers while several other male passengers built mounds of snow, fifty yards to the front and rear of the coach. A wheel rim was stuck into the mounds to warn others, at dusk. When an oil container under the coach has to be moved on the snow, you get the same effect as pouring water on acid. It sprays everywhere. I managed to get a few burns over my face and all over my clothes. Luckily the burns have just about healed. It's not the cold on my body that worries me, it's my frozen fingers and toes that become numb and painful, regardless of wearing warm clothing and gloves.

John dismantled part of the pump and found the rubber diaphragm had split, probably caused by pumping near solid diesel. He installed a spare diaphragm, drained some diesel out of the tank and rigged up a drip feed from inside the coach. We then drove off towards Shirvan, approximately twenty km away.

About this time a police car from Shirvan arrived, siren and lights flashing. They had probably been told about our peril by a passing motorist. The police took John to town for water. Once he returned, away we went, stopping every kilometre or two to top-up the radiator because the bottom half was frozen. The guy filling the radiator spilled some water on his jacket, and the drips froze before he had time to brush them off. The coach limped into Shirvan, with the guy pouring diesel into the funnel, with the gas stove on the dashboard melting ice on the windscreen while John had his head out the window, trying to see. The radiator was boiling, despite the antifreeze. It was quite an experience.

We spent three nights in the small town of Shirvan while the coach was being repaired. John recovered slightly, having put in a brilliant effort in terrible conditions, not to mention feeling ill from swallowing diesel as well. The locals were quite surprised as this was an unexpected visit. We were curiosities, what with our right-hand drive English coach and unusual items such as rucksacks.

One of the girls on the coach, Pauline, had an empty whisky bottle filled with water. It froze solid and shattered. She was also worried that her full bottle of whiskey had shattered but fortunately it hadn't. However, a TCP disinfectant bottle in my rucksack did freeze solid, and shattered.

I haven't mentioned much about the locals in past letters, so here goes. The Iranian men, though not all, are like animals at times. It's their upbringing. They stand outside the coach and stare in the windows at the girls. The girls get a hard time of it with being followed and pinched on the behind. I tell you, it's great being a male. We can go anywhere at will.

Groups of men stand in the streets in the towns whereas the women don't participate in local doings. The women have no liberation at all. I learnt second-hand from some American Peace Corps boys in Shirvan that in Iranian homes, the women bring the food to the door of the men's room, knock on the door and leave the food outside. When a man is in the street with his wife, he doesn't speak to his friends. In the shops, only men work. I haven't met any women in any of these recently visited countries, not since Austria. The women wear shawls, which they pull over their faces when you are approaching them in the streets. Many of the girls turn away. Tinned food is available in a limited amount and can be bought in the shops, for a price. I have noticed a lot of Australian Kraft Cheddar in tins. Most food is bought in bulk by the kilo or 100 gm lots. Varieties of nuts are sold everywhere. You notice different foods are plentiful in some towns and not in others. Milk is not common except in cities and is not recommended in Afghanistan – the cows have TB and the milk isn't pasteurised. In the streets, handicrafts are displayed on the pavements together with handmade tools. It is simply fascinating.

On the morning of the ninth in Shirvan, we all rose early for the long trip to Herat, in Afghanistan. Do you think that the coach would start? The electrolyte in the battery must have frozen and all attempts to heat it up failed. After pushing the coach in the streets of the town in an attempt to start it, a passing jeep gave it a push start. An hour and a half later, the journey recommenced. John's special mixture of kerosene and diesel was really making her purr as well as stopping the diesel from freezing. We reached the Afghan border just before dusk and kept our fingers crossed we would get through before it closed for the night. After completing the usual formalities, we headed for Herat.

Indigo's brochure stated that the road is not to be travelled by night due to the danger of bandits. John warned us that if anything happened, to hit the deck. He turned the showcase lights off to disguise us as a truck because bandits simply love buses. I certainly didn't sleep over that section of road and figured it was going to be a bandit's life rather than mine if it came to a showdown.

On the road ahead, people were standing on either side waving us down. An obvious ambush! John continued straight ahead and we arrived safely in Herat. On this subject, fifteen tourists have been murdered in the area in the last three months – mainly French. Apparently the French make a lot of trouble and don't get on too well here. They usually have their hearts cut out.

On the road into the town our driver pointed out towers on which bodies used to be hung, probably for religious reasons. I expected Herat to be a big city full of paved streets and concrete like Iran and Iraq, but this country is just so different. The most interesting on this trip I would say.

John's favourite countries are Afghanistan and Nepal. He reckons the Afghans are probably the nicest people he's met.

The men have such similar appearances, it's uncanny. They lead hard lives working long hours, which shows in their faces. They look so serious. The children are really nice, just like the Bedouin in Jordan.

On arrival in Herat, one boy dressed in rags kept pointing towards the bucket of rubbish in the coach. We didn't wake up to why he wanted it until we gave it to him. The boy emptied it on the road and a mad scramble followed for the contents. It's heartbreaking. It's impossible to feed them all. I gave one ragged child a piece of mandarin and the look of thanks I received was really heart-warming. There has been a drought in Afghanistan for four years, so imagine the scene.

The hotel/restaurant was a simple, wonderful place with rooms running off a corridor. Logs used as beams are exposed in the roofs, and the whole place is a nice cosy affair for 40 Afghans a night (currency) – (74 – 78 Afghans equal US\$1 or 180 Afghans = 1 pound Sterling).

It's the cleanest hotel yet on the trip, and was a shame to leave.

On the subject of money the banks only change travellers cheques while the black market changes cash. At the border, travellers cheques got a better rate than cash, which is unusual and the border gave a better rate than in the towns.

The restaurant at the hotel serves good cheap meals and the payment is based on honesty. You pay the man on the desk for whatever you had and he doesn't seem to keep tabs on who has and hasn't paid. Wouldn't it be nice if this worked in the rest of the world! The people are so nice and helpful, I wouldn't dream of ripping them off.

This country is semi-lawless, as you will have gathered. Hash, flick knives, guns – no questions asked. I've examined flick knives in the streets. One had a knuckle duster hand grip as well. It's frightening to think what happens when the button is pressed accidentally. No licences needed for pistols either. One I could have bought for US$6 was a fountain pen type. That took a single 22 calibre cartridge. Some of the men did buy pistols and shoulder holsters in the hope of getting licences later. In the streets, kids continually want to sell us hashish. It's ok for them to smoke it but illegal to sell to foreigners. One guy offered me a solid lump the shape and size of a cake of Camay. My eyes popped. He wanted 300 Afghans for it. I offered 100 Afghans. (Before I say anything more – understand this – I often bargain for something regardless of whether I want it or not.) Another kid translated and spoke to the dealer then told me he buys it for 150 Afghans and wants 50 Afghans commission. The next thing I saw was a uniformed guy approaching, so I said, "No, we don't want the coach washed." The officer proceeded to question them about what they were selling, found the dope and took the kid away somewhere. I cannot begin to imagine what the lump he showed me would be worth in Australia.

About five of us had boots made in a little shop in Herat for 450 Afghans a pair. The same item at home would cost many times more. The little man stayed up all night to get them finished in time. I need them for the rest of the trip and at home they should be good for going rabbit shooting, etc. Two girls bought Afghan coats but I doubt they will get them through Australian customs.

Something I must mention is what grand horse and carriage taxis they have. The timber buggies are in beautiful condition. The wooden wheels are polished and varnished, and the axle-to-body springs are chromed. The white horses carry red plumes on their bridles. To see the horse trotting or cantering with bells jingling, according to the motion, is simply grand. Watching the shadow of the horse and buggy together with the jingle, while the horse is doing a fast trot when all is quiet at midnight, and not forgetting the sound of the hooves and cartwheels, is a wonderful and colourful sight.

***

13th January1973

Kandahar – what a change from Herat! It is a grotty place indeed. The locals try to rip us off. Meat hangs in open shops, dragging on the ground, covered in flies. Some Afghans try to lure you into shops. One guy offered us 80 Afghans to the dollar when everywhere else it's 74–76. When Peter and I saw the dark passageway into the shop we decided that the risk wasn't worthwhile. Luckily, on the outskirts of the town we found a really clean pastry shop that was making apple pie! I think that all of *Indigo's* passengers must have made a beeline for that shop. The pie was full of apple, not like shops in Aussie. Boy, what a treat! Look out mum when I get home. I won't stop eating and drinking milk for a week. We are so well-off in Australia that we take good food for granted.

Weather conditions in Kandahar were good. Beautiful sunshine during the day but as we head north to Kabul, we can expect snow and generally colder conditions. The cold at this latitude is ok. No wind makes it quite pleasant.

I'm not much for souvenirs, particularly when I know I'll have to carry them later. At the moment my pack is light, especially compared with others. They carry all sorts of unnecessary items. I saw some really nice silk in Damascus being hand-woven and was tempted to buy four metres. At 22 Syrian pounds, approximately A$4 a metre, it's cheap, but I've decided to wait until I get to Thailand and have a look there.

At this stage I don't know whether I'll be flying home from Singapore, going by boat or island-hopping. Blue is now flying out of Kathmandu to Sydney due to lack of finances. I hope others don't follow suit. Even though we are having a good time, it's a long time to be travelling on a coach. We will all be glad to get to Kathmandu and hopefully begin new adventures.

A new girl called Andrea has joined the trip. She's an Aussie from Adelaide and the only decent bit of talent on the coach. Our courier, an American girl of nineteen who was disliked by all, was given the bullet in Lebanon. Felicity, a dumb twenty-year-old, left the trip in Herat to continue to Kabul with a guy she had only just met, and then to Kathmandu on her own. No common sense at all! She certainly picked the most dangerous countries to travel alone in. It might be alright for a man, but not a frail girl with a build like Twiggy. The previous courier also had the habit of making friends with all the freaks she met in hotels, too.

We left Kandahar at 8.00am, heading for Kabul. Today is Christmas Day for Afghanistan so we expect a lot of Kabul to be closed down. The celebration period is over six days. At this stage we are about a week behind schedule due to our detour to Israel and the breakdown. The border between Pakistan and India is open one day a week, Thursday I think, so we don't have to rush. It was a long drive from Herat to Kandahar across barren, monotonous plains. I kept falling asleep because of the unchanging scenery and the drone of the engine.

Not far from Kandahar the unthinkable happened. The coach ran out of diesel. A passing local bus stopped to give aid, draining diesel into our tank. The passengers on the local bus consisted of young men who quickly dispersed on the road. Much to our surprise and delight, forming a circle, they started to clap and dance. So here we were out in the middle of nowhere, and this happened! Such friendly, happy people too.

***

14th January 1973

We arrived in Kabul fairly early yesterday afternoon after a boring drive across barren country. Much of Afghanistan is like this, but I believe they have a good area north of here where most of the fruit is grown. The tangerines are really plentiful and cheap although there appears to be a shortage of many vegetables. The road leading into Kabul took us through mud and filth. You have to see the conditions to believe them, however the section of town where we are staying is not too bad. It's much easier to adapt to the conditions having done it gradually moving through various countries. The surrounding streets contain shops selling furs, souvenirs, antiques, rugs, shirts, Afghan-type coats, lapidary work, etc. I'm glad I don't buy on impulse as I would be broke. At this stage I have 90 pounds Sterling in travellers cheques and US$60 cash, with about 150 pounds Sterling to pick up in Nepal from the cancelled airline ticket. So I might be ok.

It looks as though we may be delayed in Kabul. One of the passengers, Sue, needs a Pakistan and India visa, but with the Muslim Christmas, embassies are not open. John also wants to get papers for the coach fixed up here as it will be a lot less hassle than in Lahore. If we arrive in Kathmandu a fortnight late, we may miss out on Kashmir and the houseboats in India, which would have been a highlight of the trip. However, things might change.

I've been telling different people in our group about your century temperatures at home and they tell me to shut up. It gets very cold here and everyone is envious. We tease one another about different kinds of food we wish we had, such as a good old meat pie and a can of Fosters. We all talk about what our return to Australia is going to be like. For me, it's into the nearest pub in Darwin and a nice cold schooner. Gee, we really miss these simple things, and the sun and surf. The trip seems like a long time, even though it's only six months tomorrow.

***

15 January 1973

Had a meeting yesterday afternoon to discuss pressing on into Pakistan this afternoon, leaving Sue behind to collect her Indian visa, then fly to India to catch us up. Pending the linings on the coach being replaced today, we shall leave this afternoon, spend the night in a town near the border, then cross Pakistan in twenty hours, a distance of about 500 miles to the Indian border. As I mentioned before, the border is open on Thursdays and possibly Wednesdays. If we cross on the set date we shall not lose a week, thereby enabling us to visit Kashmir.

Yesterday, while John, Blue and I were out in the street, a Japanese guy came riding by on a monobike. He stopped and turned right around on the spot, got off and came over to talk briefly. Last night he came into the hotel restaurant with his bike and entered into a conversation with a few of our mob. He is on a world trip and has been away for two years so far. He produced photographs and press cuttings from all over the world of this and his previous round the world trip, which took three years riding a conventional pushbike. He has one photograph taken of the White House in the background, between his legs, so it looks like he is sh*****g on the White House! He speaks several languages and was extremely interesting to listen to.

I have stocked up with food for Pakistan and India. They have good shops here for tinned food although it's mainly imported. The good old Kraft Cheddar tins are in the shops too.

Well I seem to be running out of conversation.

Love to you all, Ron.

Melanoma

In 1997 I was diagnosed with malignant melanoma. I had been attending a skin specialist but had lost faith in him. Twice he had frozen off an elongated 'freckle' on my right hand, which had strangely appeared halfway between my thumb and forefinger. Some months later a shiny round mole surfaced near the knuckle. I knew enough about skin cancers to know that if there was a change, get it checked, so I sought a referral to another dermatologist.

As a small child I had white-blonde hair and very fair skin. I can remember being severely sunburnt when I was in kindergarten. Blisters covered my forearms from wrist to elbow. I was also badly sunburnt as a teenager. Skin damage was inevitable.

I duly attended the referred dermatologist and related my story. She, in turn, excised the mole and sent it off to pathology. I should have been better emotionally prepared for the result, but I wasn't. The pathology showed malignancy and could I please come and see her the following day. Everyone handles unpleasant news differently and I remember sitting there, blankly looking at my hand. Shock was sitting at the periphery of my emotions but I was too scared to let it in, defying the tears at the back of my eyes to spill. I looked around. Everything in the office was normal. I didn't feel normal. I sat there in a trance-like state – numb.

I returned to the dermatologist the following day and she explained that because of the way the tumour had presented, she couldn't excise it any further. I would have to attend the South Perth Surgi Centre for the complete excision but would have to wait until this wound healed.

One week later I attended the Surgi Centre and after relaying the story to the surgeon, photos were taken and the usual medical details obtained. The doctor then explained the procedure. Because of new techniques, flesh would be excised, my hand would be dressed and I could return home. The sample would be sent off to pathology and I was to return the following day. If the edges weren't clear, more excision would take place. The doctor also advised that, depending on the wound, I may have to have a skin graft. This did not excite me at all! I was also to keep my hand upright at all times. Being right-handed, this was going to be tricky.

I was living in Subiaco and as my partner had to return to his job in the Pilbara I had to get myself to South Perth on public transport. It was cool weather and the only decent shoes I had was a pair of boots, with laces. Trying to tie the laces was extremely difficult, as every time I put my right hand down it would throb, mercilessly. The dressings also impeded the tying. I caught the train into the city and made my way to the ferry terminal. Back on land in South Perth I headed off on my 2 km walk but after several hundred yards the laces on my right boot came undone and I was worried they might trip me up. I espied a tradie sitting in his ute with the driver's door open. He was eating his lunch and enjoying the quiet view across the river. Would I dare? I approached him and asked him would he mind tying my shoelaces. He looked at me with a quizzical grin.

"Sure", he said, "so what's this all about?"

I explained, and he was very sympathetic, tying both shoelaces with double knots so they wouldn't come undone again. I was just hopeful that good news was coming my way.

To my chagrin, the doctor informed me that the edges weren't clear and he would have to take more. To say I was disappointed is an understatement, but knew I should be thankful for the process as this was, after all, saving my life.

Day three, my daughter Melanie drove me to the clinic. She chose to wait downstairs in the cafeteria. As I walked away, she joked, "Ah, they won't graft you today Mum!" I just looked back and smiled, feeling confident a graft wouldn't be necessary. The girls behind the front desk looked aghast when I walked in and said they were sorry to see me back again. I laughed as I was feeling positive and wasn't worried. The doctor called me in and just sat there, looking at me.

"What's wrong?" I asked, now feeling slightly perplexed

He didn't speak for a long moment. "I don't know how to tell you this, but we still haven't cleared the edges and I don't know where to go next. Tell me again where the mole appeared."

I showed him. "Ah", he said, "the patient always knows best."

He cut me again. Twenty minutes later I went down to the cafeteria to find Mel. She looked at me aghast. I think I was looking a little shaky. "Mum, what happened?" I explained and she sat there, dumbstruck. No doubt she felt she had mozzed me with her previous breezy comment.

Day four and I was over it. I had the throbbing hand from hell and just wanted it to end. Melanie drove me to the clinic and I thought the girls behind the desk were going to faint when they saw me again. I was duly called in and the *good news* was the edges were finally clear. Now for the skin graft. I had heard that skin grafts are worse than the wound, and they weren't wrong. Flesh for a graft is taken from the same side of the body as the wound. The doctor checked the inside of my upper arm and stood there shaking his head. Right where he wanted to excise the graft was a brown mole. I have *beautiful* Scottish skin – moles and freckles everywhere and he huffed and puffed as he had to find another *area*. I grimaced and said, "I know where you're going to take it from." He advised he would check me out, but in the meantime he insisted on cutting out the mole on my upper arm. What the hell! I was sore enough without more invasion.

I duly had to expose my posterior (as I knew I would) and sure enough *an area* was located. He went to work on my right buttock. Numbing the *spot* and while waiting for the anaesthetic to take effect he advised me that not all skin grafts *take* and if that was the case I would have to have another one. Of all the pain and discomfort I endured that week, this information just about did me in. I didn't want to hear this but I guess he was just keeping me advised.

He began to cut what looked like a large square – and I felt every slice. The anaesthetic had only deadened the inside of the piece, however I was beyond caring at that stage. When he lifted the *slab* off and placed it on the open wound it looked like a piece of hamburger. The graft area was treated and dressed, and the graft itself stapled to my hand. After all the dressings were completed I struggled off the theatre table and with the help of a nurse, dressed. Walking was difficult. I was shaky and light-headed. My emotions were working overtime. Melanie helped me into the lift and steadied me out to her car. Just getting into the car was a trial and by this time pain and shock had taken hold. I just sat there and cried and cried.

It took a long time to recover, more so from the wound where the graft had been taken from. There was also an emotional toll. I was fifty years old and not ready to die. The diagnosis had completely upset my equilibrium. I desperately wanted to live but knew I could get secondaries. Negative thoughts flooded my every waking hour. Now you could say I was overreacting but I don't think anyone who has ever had a cancer scare can say there haven't been times when their psyche just plummets. It took me six months to come to terms with the knowledge.

***

At the time of writing it is now 2019. In the last twenty-two years I've had seven malignant melanomas, with the seventh involving a big operation and having a node removed from my groin. I've also had several other 'nasties'. Situations such as these make you realise how lucky you are and how fantastic is the progress medical science has made. We all have to die sometime but I count my blessings that I'm still active and healthy. My advice – don't slip up on a check-up and SLIP, SLOP, SLAP!

Antarctica

In November 2018 I flew to Ushuaia on the southern coast of South America. There I joined *L'Austral*, a ship from the Ponant Line, and sailed for Antarctica following the Great Austral Loop. Many people have asked, "Why there?" My response has always been, "It's the last frontier and isolation is one aspect that always has me fascinated." Having lived in two remote areas, isolation is a solace to me. I love it!

An Expedition Team onboard was responsible for not only our welfare but also the welfare of any animals we encountered. The team was made up of botanists, biologists, ecologists, historians, wildlife experts, bird experts, and scientists. Their knowledge of the environment and the animals that inhabited the islands and the seas was stunning, and at times very entertaining.

When we encountered the sea *on the boil* it was an experience I will never forget. I was fortunate enough not to be too seasick and marvelled at the ferocity of the unencumbered waves. They were majestic. The raw power was exhilarating and at times, frightening. I was warned that if this was exciting, Drake's Passage on the return journey might test my resolve.

We visited the treeless Falkland Islands, which only receives ten days of sun per year and were lucky enough that this day was one. A 2 km walk led us to a large Albatross colony nestled into the side of massive cliffs on the opposite side of the island. Low swooping, they were a sight to behold. The cacophony was deafening.

Passing island cliffs that are 130 million-years-old, our next stop was Gritvyken which is the principal settlement on South Georgia. British owned, it is a pretty little town which was once a large whaling station. The wind was icy but the scenery was stunning. Penguins and seals lined the stony beaches. Two snow-capped mountains were a majestic backdrop with two glaciers visible. A swirling black cloud coated the first mountain. Due to the forces of nature it was difficult to discern whether the mountain had captured the clouds, or the clouds had captured the mountain. It constantly drifted, coating the peaks and just as it seemed the mountain had shed its ghostly coat, the cloud would return to smother the peaks with its swirling, misty skirts.

There is an interesting Post Office and store in the little town. It also has an amazing museum full of history, much of it relating to Sir Ernest Shackleton, whose final resting place is in the local cemetery. Gritvyken is where Shackleton planned the rescue of his crew from the stricken vessel *Endurance* in 1915.

A picturesque white Whalers' Church nestles at the base of huge snow-capped mountains. Rusted remnants of whale oil processing plants and abandoned whaling ships dot the shoreline. Hundreds of bleached whale bones lie scattered everywhere and make good scratching points for fur seals. Penguins waddle nonchalantly, navigating the pitted shoreline and the tourists.

In the course of the cruise, we were treated to fin whales, killer whales, humpbacks and minkes. We also saw elephant seals, hundreds of fur seals and birds galore. Among the penguin species there were king penguins, adelie, chinstrap and gentoo. The penguins are so used to tourists, their curiosity and trust is humbling.

On 30th November we were up early for iceberg sightings as we were now officially in Antarctic waters. The air outside was freezing. A57A is a massive iceberg that broke away from the

Antarctic shelf in 2011. It is twenty kilometres long, nine kilometres wide and thirty kilometres high (but above water you can only see approximately one-seventh of its actual height). It is magnificent! Caves and stunning blue grottos undermine parts of its waterline base. Details of the face look like someone has sliced bits off a huge meringue. It is said it would keep Paris in fresh water for 300 years. Everyone was spellbound.

The final day before returning to Ushuaia we were lucky enough to step ashore on to the actual Antarctic continent. The day was cool/cold. Thick, puffy clouds rendered the landscape white, blue-grey and gun-metal grey. Even so, this did nothing to dampen everyone's enthusiasm. Riding the zodiacs through the brash ice, watching penguins scale impossible ice cliffs, encountering free-floating icebergs with their beautiful blue grottos and seeing ice tumble off a glacier are memories cast indelibly in my mind.

On shore, we followed the red flags laid out by the Expedition Team and climbed a snow-covered hill which afforded 360° views. The scene was serene. The pristine remoteness and ambience were both humbling and exhilarating. The silence deafening!

Back on board, the Captain set sail at a leisurely pace. No-one wanted to leave and everyone was soaking up as much of the ice and snow-clad scenery as possible.

We weren't on board long when the call went out there were orcas (killer whales) swimming close to the port side. Whenever the whale call came, there was always a stampede of bodies vying for the best vantage points on deck. Exiting the cabin, the 'Bird Man', George, raced past me yelling, "They're at the back of the ship. Run!" I did.

It is impossible to describe the exhilaration of what unfolded. The whales, which had been swimming very close to port, disappeared. A few minutes later they surfaced and 'sat' adjacent to the disembarkation platform. There was a large male, four females and a young calf *lolling* up next to its father and rolling in somersaults. The whales would sometimes sink out of sight, then come up blowing, watching us watching them. This scenario continued for approximately fifteen minutes. Everyone was gobsmacked, excited, overcome, flabbergasted! Petra, the botanist, could barely believe her eyes. She said they had never witnessed this before and explained this type of whale behaviour meant the animals were very relaxed. It was an amazing privilege!

Returning to Ushuaia we had to cross the Drake Passage, which is the narrow stretch of water separating South America from the Antarctic Peninsula. Eight metre waves crashed over the bow for approximately thirty-six hours. We were all in lockdown. Being on the lower deck and watching the bottle green walls of water slamming into the cabin window occasionally took my breath away. The velocity of the *hit* was breathtaking.

The most unforgettable memories of Antarctica are the pristine landscape and the sound of silence.

Hong Kong

One of the items on my bucket list in 2013 was to sail *somewhere* on the QE11. The Cunard Line happened to be selling portions of an around-the-world cruise, i.e., embark here, disembark where you will. I discussed the idea with my friend, who was uninterested. However, the advertisement kept popping into my head. The portion of the trip I was keen on was from Singapore to Hong Kong. It was an eight-day voyage stopping at ports in Thailand and Vietnam. Not being a huge cruise fan, eight days sounded just about right. I love Hong Kong and one of my cousins currently lived there.

In passing, I happened to mention the cruise to my neighbour. Win's husband had passed away in the previous twelve months. Showing her the advertisement I said, "One day, you and I might do something like this."

Her response was, "Oh, we will."

The following Monday I was busy at work when I received a phone call from Win. After brief pleasantries she said to me, "Can you please call the Travel Agent and give her your credit card?"

"My credit card? Why do I need to call a Travel Agent to give her my credit card?"

"Well I don't have any money on my credit card and she needs the deposit."

"The deposit?"

"Yes, for the trip."

"What trip?"

"The trip on the QE11!"

For several seconds I couldn't speak. My brain went into overdrive, and the coloured flashing lights didn't seem to connect with any functioning brain waves. I believe I stammered, "Do you have the Travel Agent's phone number?" It was promptly supplied. It took a few minutes for me to catch my breath. I had no idea what date the ship was sailing from Singapore to Hong Kong and didn't know if I could apply for the leave.

I made the phone call. I explained the situation and said I would need twenty-four hours to think about it. The Agent wasn't too impressed but I needed time to digest the information. Needless to say the rest of the day was a bit of a blur.

When I arrived home, I spoke to my friend about the cruise and again he showed little interest. I got the giggles. When he asked what was funny my response was, "Well you're not going on the cruise, but I am!" After enlightening him of the situation, we both had a good laugh and agreed it would be a good thing to do.

On the appointed date Win and I flew to Singapore. We spent two days sightseeing, then boarded the QE11 and sailed for Hong Kong. The ship was magnificent and we indulged ourselves in everything that was on offer. When we arrived at the Thai port, most of the passengers disembarked, which allowed us free rein. Win had never been in a spa pool, so we changed into our bathers and headed for the stern. By the time I dragged her out she looked like a cooked prune. She loved the spa and didn't want to leave!

After arriving in Hong Kong, we moved to a hotel, as we were flying home from there.

The following morning, I desperately wanted to find a chemist who sold a particularly good hand cream. Win and I trawled the streets and, eventually finding the product, I indulged in several tubes.

Navigating our way back to the hotel we noticed a large flotilla of cruise ships had docked during the night. Walking down a side street, I heard a Scottish accent. It was coming from a woman who was talking to an Indian gentleman outside a tailor's shop. Being intent on finding my way back to our hotel, the accent barely registered. Rounding a corner, I suddenly spun on a sixpence and retraced my steps. Tapping the Scottish lady on the shoulder I said, "What are you doing here Agnes?"

Agnes and I had worked together as secretaries for many years at the Royal Agricultural Society of WA. We were good friends. Agnes turned. She stood there, mouth open, staring. Agnes's husband Stuart burst out laughing and said, "That's the first time I've seen you lost for words, for years!" Everyone just cracked up. They had arrived with friends on a cruise ship during the night and were staying at a hotel around the corner from us.

Of all the street corners in Hong Kong, this was 'one for the books'!

The People Watcher

Another short story. This one inspired by a writing group exercise about someone having a coughing fit. The brief insisted that we create a whole scene and so I found myself in a café with this poor soul.

One summer's day as I was revising notes from my writing class and sitting quietly at the back of my favourite restaurant in Leederville, I saw a man enter through the double doors and earnestly look around. He looked slightly uncomfortable. A waitperson approached and then turned on her heel and walked in my direction, the wooden floorboards creaking under the pressure and the lazy ceiling fans thrumming their own tune overhead. I can't really say why I kept looking at the man following her, but as they drew closer I dropped my eyes to the page so as not to appear as though I was staring.

A table was selected after a small moment of choice and he seated himself with his back to the wall. He had a view to both the left and right, as well as straight ahead at the old station clock with roman numerals that graced the opposite wall. He carried a leather bag, which hung from a long strap over his shoulder. He placed the bag on the floor beside him and as he turned back to the table, he glanced my way. I noticed he had one of those faces that is uneven, in that the left-hand side of his face was collapsed in, whereas the right-hand side was much fuller.

Because of the hour, the restaurant was only half full, which made my surreptitious scrutiny slightly more difficult. There was something about this man that held my curiosity. Although the day was cool for summer, he was dressed in a brown plaid jacket with a cream coloured shirt and a patterned tan tie. His slacks were a lighter brown and looked to be of a heavier cloth. His shoes were also tan and I could see that one sock was dark-brown. His hair was black and he wore heavy black-rimmed glasses.

He made a quick cursory glance at the menu and summoned the waiter. I was interested to know what he ordered. Because of his quick selection it appeared he may have eaten here on other occasions.

Trying to concentrate on my notes was becoming increasingly difficult. I love people watching but because of the quite small distance between us, I didn't want to appear rude. His meal duly arrived, which was a mushroom and spinach pasta and a large latte. He attacked the pasta with great gusto and I was spellbound watching his Adam's apple, which was quite pronounced, bob up and down hitting his shirt collar and then disappearing up under his chin. It looked like a ping-pong ball being rapidly bounced and it held me transfixed. His concentration on his meal was such that he ate quickly, as though he was either very hungry or just in a hurry to finish the meal.

I was trying to work out where he came from and what was his role in life. He didn't look like your average 'suit' from the city. If anything he looked slightly out of place. Was he an on-road salesman, if they still exist? He didn't look a bit like a used-car salesman. My impression was he was not particularly a 'people person'.

By this time I couldn't focus on my notes. To shift my attention I got up and walked to the door of the restaurant, intimating to the waitperson that I would return shortly. The sky was the beautiful blue that we are so used to in Perth. No clouds were visible, but a slight, cool breeze swept along the footpath with just enough momentum to scurry some leaves in front of it. The usual flotsam and jetsam of traffic buzzed along Oxford Street, which no-one particularly noticed, until a hot pink Porsche screeched out of Newcastle Street and then lazily, knowing it was on show, cruised towards the lights at Vincent Street, the driver smugly smirking. I half-thought he might wave, such was his bonhomie.

Before returning to my table I requested another cappuccino. I needed something to keep me at my table to continue my observations. On sitting down I glanced over to the customer in question and was surprised to see him with an open folder on the table and he was busily writing or correcting something. My curiosity had my intellectual juices flowing. What was he doing? There was a calculator next to the folder and every now and again he would punch numbers into it, then scribble on the page. His thought process was in full swing as you could see the intense concentration on his lopsided face.

Without warning, he began choking. Throwing down his pen he scrambled for the glass of water on the table. In his haste he knocked the glass over, which then hit the water bottle and both crashed to the floor. His face was turning crimson as he struggled for air. I jumped up and ran towards him, yelling at the staff for help. Most people sat idly at their tables, however two men got up and hurried towards us. Because I reached him first I was hitting his back between his shoulder blades in a frantic effort to help. Fortunately one of the men had some medical knowledge and managed to slide in behind the man's chair, wrap his arms around his torso and pull backwards and upwards. A strangled gasp was followed by more coughing, with tears streaming down his face and saliva dripping from his bottom lip. A waiter placed another glass of water near his shaking hand. He tentatively took a small sip, gasping as the water slid down his throat. I pulled out the chair next to his and sat, placing my hand on his arm for reassurance.

Understandably he took several moments to gain his equilibrium and sat there looking embarrassed and unsure. A waiter began clearing the broken glass and, checking that he was ok, the men returned to their tables. I stayed put. Because of my earlier observations, in a strange sort of way I felt responsible for him and quietly reassured him he was going to be alright. A small gratified smile crossed his face as he thanked me for my concern. I quietly picked up his wet papers from the table, gave them a small shake to dislodge any droplets and glanced at what I held. He was a maths teacher, marking exam papers.

Cape Lambert

In 2006, after eleven years of working at the Royal Agricultural Society of Western Australia I applied for a position as an administrator with a firm of German engineers. They designed stackers, reclaimers and shiploaders for the mining industry.

The job change was nerve-wracking. I had moved away from my comfort zone, from what was basically a large 'family', into the big wide world of commerce and industry. My boss had apparently resigned his position as sales manager and candidates were being interviewed to fill the role. This was disconcerting. I had no experience in the field and this department had to put together tenders for BHP Billiton, Rio Tinto and subsequently, Fortescue Metals. I felt all at sea, hopeful the new boss would know what he was doing.

Interestingly enough, I discovered very quickly that I couldn't relate to many of the male employees even though they were pleasant enough and very helpful. Having come from the RAS where my role was centred around everything rural, this new high-tech machine-based life left me feeling like a complete clot. My boss and his offsider dressed in suits. To begin with the whole atmosphere was quite formal. Not being super confident with the very modern computers, my lack of knowledge and skills with this upmarket equipment only added to my feelings of total inadequacy.

Machine drawings littered the desk opposite but the chair was always vacant. I was advised that a chap by the name of Darryl occupied the desk when in the office, but currently he was away onsite.

Everyone knows it takes time to settle into a new job. But how does one look busy when there's absolutely nothing to do and everyone around you is too busy to spend any time with you. My boss kept promising to talk to me about the mound of filing. When he eventually got around to it one week before he departed, he spent all of twenty minutes in a very manic session of totally inadequate explanations. He then expected me to pick up and run with documents that meant absolutely zilch to me.

He informed everyone at his farewell bash that the reason he was leaving was because I had just joined! This actually set the scene for all the ribbing and friendly banter that was to become the next ten years of my life.

My saving grace from total exasperation was that Darryl turned up one day accompanied by another bloke, named Chris. Darryl was dressed in a pair of jeans that looked like they hadn't been washed, ever! He had on a khaki shirt and sported an incredibly tanned, craggy face with shoulder-length wavy, grey-flecked hair that looked like it had been blow-dried with a wind machine. He also sported an earring. Darryl was ok and a revelation – I could relate to him.

And then there was Chris. Chris wore a used-to-be-white T-shirt, which revealed 'tatts' on his arms, baggies, and thongs, and he slopped up and down the passage always with a cheeky grin saying, 'how're ya goin'? Are ya gettin' there?" Chris had been a shearer and a plumber and he knew horses. He was ok too! After three weeks of suits 'n ties I finally felt like there were some 'real' people in the office and I began to relax.

My new boss arrived. We didn't take long to click because I rode a scooter and he rode a motorbike so we actually had something in common. It gave us something to talk about that helped break the 'newbie' ice.

Our first tender was due within the month. Chaos reigned. The previous boss hadn't done any work towards the tender, leaving us totally in the dark. Fortunately a few of the other administrators were able to offer some verbal assistance. No-one was surprised we weren't successful. There was, however, a strong belief that we wouldn't have won the contract anyway.

We slowly settled into our roles and I began to be fascinated with the machines. Having had the opportunity to eventually watch a video of a stacker and bucket wheel in operation, I lived in hope that one day I would be able to see them working 'in the field'.

Several months later, that day dawned. One of the site administrators was required to take leave, but there was no-one to fill her role within the company. I had made it known that I was keen to go to site so I suddenly became 'it'! My Personal Protective Equipment (PPE) was ordered, which included a hard hat and steel-capped boots and I then found myself winging my way to Karratha to fill the role of administrator at Cape Lambert. There was a shutdown for a bucket wheel change-out. Having had no hand-over or any practical experience, I hit the ground running. In hindsight, floundering would probably have been a better description.

I had been given a computer (that subsequently didn't work remotely), no mobile phone was supplied and being a total novice I hadn't thought to make a list of staff mobile numbers. I just *assumed* I would always be accompanied by some of my fellow workers.

Having caught the very early plane, I arrived in Karratha and 'my boss on site' met me and drove several kilometres out of town, to the camp. The camp itself was well laid out with the creamy-white dongas, and kitchen and laundry amenities set in a large expanse of red, dusty dirt. The weather was so much warmer than Perth. As I had dressed warmly for the cool morning I soon needed to shed some clothing. Once I checked into the camp I was given my room key and told to hurry up, get changed and report back to the car park. Haste was essential, but as we all know, in unfamiliar situations, haste isn't always your best friend. Once changed, I grabbed my backpack and raced to the mess to grab some crib. The construction site was some three km from the camp through low undulating hills covered in thick spinifex. The intense blue sky was endless. The site was situated right on the tip of the Cape which meant the ocean and bays surrounded us in a 90° arc. A large wharf disappeared into the ocean for several hundred metres with a conveyor belt running its length. The rich red iron ore was trundled along the belt where it could be loaded onto the ships that were berthed. This was a 24/7 process with up to eighteen ships standing off the coast at any one time, looking like a flotilla of warships waiting for the signal to advance.

The following morning I was to catch the bus to site with the day shift. My boss informed me he would let the driver know to pick up one extra when the night shift was dropped off. Feeling nervous and out of place, I made sure I was on time at the appointed place. I hadn't met most of the guys so didn't know names or faces. The bus pulled up, the night shift fell out, the day shift jumped in and the bus took off like a jet plane, spraying me with stones and grit as it vanished in a cloud of filthy red dust. What the hell! I stood there in disbelief. Hadn't the boss told him to pick me up? Just because I wasn't standing huddled with the guys, I wasn't that far away. Now what?

I had a conundrum. No phone and I didn't know anyone. Where do I go? Who do I need to speak to? I returned to the mess hoping someone could advise me what to do. Did they care? Not really! Eventually one of the chefs pointed to the Administration Office and advised me to speak to someone there.

Have you ever been in a situation where you feel helpless and hopeless? This was one of those moments. I *assumed* that because it was the Admin Office, someone there would know my boss and have his phone number. On a list. Next to a name. Wrong!

"What's his phone number?"

"I don't know."

"Sorry luv. If you don't know his number how the hell are we supposed to know it?"

"So, how do I get to site?"

"You can walk. It's about three km that way."

"Does the road lead directly to the site?"

"Well, yes and no. There are other roads that branch off."

"So how do I know which road to take?"

"You don't. There aren't any signs. Everyone here knows how to get there."

I could feel tears pricking the backs of my eyes, just waiting for me to give the nod to let them spill. Frustration was paramount.

"I don't know what to do."

"Sorry luv, can't help ya."

I stepped outside. The morning was already promising to be a scorcher. Flies buzzed like drones around my face. I had no idea where to turn. The door behind me opened and the admin guy suggested I go to the front gate to see if they could assist. Maybe they could help me cadge a lift. I nodded and walked off. Shattered. I had been so looking forward to this trip and it had turned into a big fat mess!

I arrived at the gate and explained my situation. The guys there just looked at me.

"So, what you need to do is, when you see someone you know, just jump in with them."

"I don't know anyone. I've just arrived."

"Mmm. Well, most of the vehicles will be full anyway, but if you see a spare seat, grab it."

I was struggling with the 'care factor' here.

I waited. Most vehicles were full. I was too timid to ask if I did see an empty seat.

Twenty minutes passed and I was still standing there. The gate people had all but vanished.

I was at the point of thinking I would return to my room to see if my boss would actually bother to come looking for me, when a beat-up old blue vehicle pulled up. The driver was not in site gear. He was very tanned and covered in tatts, wearing a navy blue singlet and dirty jeans. Dare I?

"Excuse me. Are you going to site?" Dumb question. He's not in site gear.

"No luv, I'm not. What's the problem?"

I explained.

"Mmm. Well, I'm actually going into the town."

He obviously noticed my crestfallen look.

To spice things up, the Gate Supervisor came out and bawled at the driver, "Move!"

After a moment's hesitation the driver said, "Jump in." So I did.

The inside of the car looked like a tip and as we exited the gate he took off, spraying dust and stones in a big wheelie. Great! What had I got myself into? I actually felt scared. I was in an unfamiliar place speeding down a windy road with a bloke I didn't know. The chat seemed ok, but was it ok? For some reason I suddenly had visions of being found bum-up in the spinifex, if I was ever found at all. I wanted out, but then I thought if I showed panic that might not be the best idea either. After what seemed like an eternity, but was probably only twenty minutes, the site gate came into view. Relief washed over me like a tidal wave.

Thanking the driver, I jumped out and approached the gate.

"Sorry luv, you can't come in without an escort."

"What?"

"You need an escort."

I needed to hit someone!

"Can you please ring my boss so he can come and get me."

"Ring him yerself."

A deep sigh permeated the periphery of my mind.

"I don't have a phone."

"What? Who comes to site without a bloody phone."

"I do", I yelled, as I thumped the desk. "I wasn't issued with a phone. Please can you help?"

A long stare!

"What's your boss's name?"

I advised his name and the shutdown we were on.

"Don't have no-one by that name. Don't know 'im."

Exasperation. Frustration. Deprivation. Isolation. How much more of this could I take?

A site vehicle pulled up and my boss got out.

"Where the bloody hell have you been?"

I gawped at him. Now I really was going to hit someone.

"Oh, well THANK YOU very much," I roared. "How dare you? I asked you to tell the driver to make sure to pick me up this morning and he bloody well sprayed me with stones and dirt and drove away without me. I was right there," I snapped, then self-righteously straightened my skewed Princess tiara and berated him regarding my hideous morning.

"Chook, get in. And just settle, will ya!"

After another fifteen-minute drive we arrived at the scungiest looking site offices I have ever seen. The place looked like a bombsite. This was *home* for the next week.

It was an interesting week. The bus driver apologised. Bill had told him to pick me up but the driver forgot. He never forgot again, because I never let him! Of the three computers that our office had issued, only the boss's worked. The remotes for the other two failed. This created massive problems as I was required by the Client to keep the worksheets up-to-date. I was also required to look after the admin for our office, plus a thousand other things that no-one else wanted to take responsibility for. The site engineer also needed to use the computer. The only available phone was the boss's, who never let it out of his sight. The twelve-hour days took their toll. The arguments never ceased. But, what happens onsite stays onsite.

The compelling memories of that frantic week are the camaraderie that you have with your fellow workers, warts and all. With all the differences that abound, you do actually blend together to become a team. You have to! The overall engineering, electrical, structural, mechanical and physical work that was involved was mind-blowing.

A multitude of different tradies scurrying around like ants on a honey pot.

Ships docking, being filled and departing on a never-ending rotation, tugged by an invisible cord. An eye-boggling moment when the bucket wheel was finally lifted back into place.

Walks on the rock wall that kept the sea at bay.

The smell of the sea and the gentle lapping of waves was a salve to my sometimes frayed nerves – as was the limitless blue sky.

It may have been a tough week in many respects, but I felt alive!

I went on to do four more site admin reliefs over five years. Nothing changed. No computer, no phone, no backup. It still makes me smile!

A Moment in Time

A little blend of fact and fiction – this all happened... apart from the hitchhiker.

The holidays had arrived and I was impatient to depart for my ancestral home. My career obligations had kept me absent for several years but past memories needed sating. I hastily finished my last minute packing, threw my suitcase in the boot of the car and, backing out in a hurry, almost knocked over my elderly next-door neighbour. She was standing at the letterbox cheerily waving me away.

The cloudless, cobalt blue of the sky irresistibly beckoned as I headed north, while a saucy breeze kept the morning heat under control. I was euphoric to the point where I had to watch my speed, so desperate was I to put space between myself and the city.

After refuelling at New Norcia, I was about to depart when there was a rapid knock on the passenger window. Startled, I looked sideways to observe a scrawny, middle-aged man in a rumpled jacket that was covered in a fur of dust. Flakes of desiccated skin peeled thinly off his face, which bore the ravages of windblown granite and loneliness. The skin around his eyes looked punched and was the colour of a dying flower. Grey-black greasy hair that looked like dried seaweed hung scraggily around his ears. I turned the lever on the window winder and allowed the glass to descend a couple of inches.

"Hey Girly, where ya headed?"

"Just north for a bit."

"What's a bit?"

"Just a bit further north of here."

"Don't s'pose you could give me a lift?"

"Sorry, not really. I'm in a hurry. Have to meet someone."

"If ya could just take me to a further drop-off point, I'd 'preciate it!"

Stumped, my hesitation was palpable. A silent scream ricocheted between my ears.

With a look that would encourage rising dough to capitulate, a guttural sigh uttered from him, deep within. Likewise, in a quagmire of emotional frustration, my happy thoughts collapsed like a house of cards. I felt like a discriminatory villain. Such was my confusion at being so accosted, my resolve caved in.

"Get in."

"Thanks girly. Knew ya would."

He ripped open the back door of the car with a strength that belied his looks and tossed an old canvas gunny sack on to the seat. A lidless billy was tied to the strap, enriched by years of soot. I squirmed, having recently vacuumed the car. Slamming the rear door, with an uncoordinated lurch he fell into the front seat, dragging one leg after the other in behind him. A feculent fragrance suddenly invaded my sensitive nostrils.

The rhythm of my ordered life felt disrupted and a tangible undercurrent pervaded the car as I drove out on to the Great Northern Highway. Following the hemline of the road, my head was in a whirl. Owing to the vandalism of my time I tried to maintain a vinegary sternness, which was cold salve to my jaded nerves. Surreptitiously observing my passenger, I noted his arthritic fingers and the three-day stubble lodged in the crags that pleated his face. He was part-Aboriginal.

Giving in to my diverse emotions, I had to acknowledge that now I had to put up with the situation. I had allowed this to happen and was annoyed with myself for giving in to an unwanted circumstance. In turn, his psychic evaluation of me had picked up my veiled displeasure. There was currently little democracy in the car and we drove in silence for some distance. However, not being one to harbour a self-inflicted grudge, I made a tentative effort at conversation. It opened a flood gate.

His name was Jimmy and he was a Dogger. A station manager had contacted him with a job offer. With a voice as soft as butterfly wings, so different from his original approach, he proved loquacious in a lazy sort of way. His conversation took shape like a slow-moving cloud as he gathered his thoughts. It appeared he was a connoisseur of race, and on this subject his mind was as tight as an unfurled bud as he gave vent to all the wrongs that had been done to his people, and the collateral damage of same.

With my usual wilful stubbornness, I was finding it hard to give in to the moment, but as my indignation began to subside, I relaxed into the conversation, particularly when mentioning the love of the land we were driving towards. He was heading for Wubin. As I was travelling further north, I unfolded my own story of having grown up on a sheep station. A wild, crooked grin lit up his face as memory caught him, placing him temporarily outside himself. His face relaxed. Having initially thought him pugnacious, my attitude began to soften. Here was something we had in common. What better way was there for two strangers to communicate and share something that was close to both their hearts!

"Are your people Yamatji?"

Dead silence. After several hollow minutes, I looked at him thinking he hadn't heard the question. He was gazing out the passenger window and just as I was about to ask again, he half-turned and looked at me, his visage indecipherable.

"What would you know about Yamatji?" The words rasped out of his mouth.

"The station my family owns is Yamatji country."

"Oh yeah! So what do you know about Yamatji?"

"Well, I know the Yamatji lands extend from the coastal plain and inland, covering the Murchison region. Ernie Dingo is a Yamatji man, as is Ben Wyatt, the WA Labour Party Treasurer." Silence.

To break the small impasse that ensued I mentioned a previous station owner had told us where there was the grave of an Aboriginal man, which was on the station's southern run. I also told him of an ancient breakaway carrying the name of Thewdawidgee, which lay in the furthest paddock bordering the next-door station. Here, handprints sit purple and orange on the time-ravaged, creviced rock wall. The Lands Department have a staked sign there designating the area as an Aboriginal heritage site.

Checking that my passenger was content to hear what I had to say, my inner vision took hold as I navigated the highway. I told him about the time we had gone for a walk out beyond Mudakulka Rock, which sits two km east from the homestead. This particular morning was warm with a cloudless, cornflower-blue sky. The red earth absorbed the sun's rays and threw the heat up our bare legs. Friendly bush flies were our constant companions, continuously buzzing around our ears, causing us to break off wattle switches to shoo them away. We wanted to explore that part of the station as it was inaccessible by vehicle and too thick for motorbikes. We walked for approximately half-an-hour, crossing dry seasonal creek beds and dodging huge Golden Orb spiders, which were strung throughout the Jam wattles.

Walking out from the scrub cover, a pockmarked shelf of orange granite spread out before us. It was elongated, with the usual undulations peculiar to ancient rock. It fell away from us as we crossed. Stepping over a small ridge and down the other side, we were stopped in our tracks. Charcoal remains from a fire lay on top of the flat, sun-gilded granite, along with stone axes and flints. Unburnt twigs that had been part of the fire clustered the edges of the dark charcoal stain. The scene was surreal. Serene. We were spellbound. No-one spoke. After some quiet moments of observation, we all silently moved away as one, without a word. It was as though we had intruded, uninvited, on a family's quiet afternoon gathering.

Such was the effect of our discovery we walked in silence for some distance, crossing yet another dry creek bed. Heading towards some massive boulders surrounded on the lee side by beautiful York gums, the dappled shade danced their shadows in the soft breeze on the vertical rock face. A secluded flat, grassed area, which was unusual for this type of country, lay in front of us. Again, we were astonished. The remains of mia-mias stood solitary below the gums on the grassy flat, the frame poles still holding their teepee like position. The protective covering had long gone, but here was ancient history cradled within nature, protected by the giant boulders. A small waterhole was at their base. A grinding stone sat squat beside one of the small mia-mia frames.

I looked at my passenger and saw that his eyes were moist. There was silence in the car for a short time, but I relayed to him as best I could, how much this had affected my family. It was banal to suggest it was a magic moment, as words simply could not describe the emotions we all felt. I told him how privileged we were to have discovered this, and had wondered how long it had been since another human had attended this site.

We drove on in silence. I could see a multitude of emotions criss-crossing his face and when I felt he had regained some composure, I offered to tell him some of the stories of the Aboriginal stockmen who worked the station, in the early days.

His face softened. With a small smile there was a quick nod of acceptance.

The car effortlessly chewed up the kilometres and as spokes of sunlight began to cast sharp shadows across the bitumen, the ruddy glow of a dying day brought peace to the two strangers. I said goodbye to him at Wubin in a frowning sort of admiration and wished him luck with his job.

Inwardly, this chance meeting had afforded me the opportunity to take a step back and contemplate how easy it is to make hurried judgements.

This was his country. It was also mine.

Dingle

In late April 2018 my friend and I flew to Paris as we were booked on a World War I Battlefields tour of France. My friend's grandfather had fought at the Somme and as we both had an avid interest in the two World Wars, this was added incentive.

As usual on these tours there was a mixture of nationalities that included eight Irish, all of whom were related - brothers, sisters, cousins and in-laws. They hailed from the beautiful picturesque town of Dingle on the south-west coast of southern Ireland, in County Kerry.

I had always wanted to visit Dingle. *Ryan's Daughter* was filmed there and the scenery had me captivated. My friend and I previously toured Ireland in 1997 and stayed at a cosy little bed and breakfast in Dingle for a couple of nights. The first day there we were desperate to do some washing, so as soon as breakfast was over we stuffed the *unmentionables* into a plastic bag and headed out to find a laundromat. Unbeknown to us the Irish are late risers. Very few places were open. Winding our way through the narrow, cold cobbled streets we happened upon a craft shop. There was a lass behind the counter talking with a customer, so we bided our time looking at the variety of handmade crafts.

After the customer departed the lass looked across at us and with a very Aussie accent said, "Does that bag say Perth, Perth,

Western Australia?" We got a shock as we hadn't heard her accent previously.

"Yes, it is," I replied.

There was much excitement on her behalf at having a couple of Aussies to talk to. She was originally a nurse from South Australia but was living with her Irish boyfriend, who was a farmer. Unable to secure a nursing position in Dingle she was managing the craft shop, which was a good option for her. We spent some time chatting and she said how great it was to hear an Aussie accent for a change. On that note, we exchanged a lot of laughs. When we exclaimed surprise at how everything was still closed she gave a hearty laugh and explained the Irish eat late, party long and sleep late.

Because some of our Battlefields' companions were from Dingle, I related this story to Bill, one of the Irishmen. The further I went into the story the broader Bill's smile spread across his craggy face. He let me finish and then said, "Ah yes, that would be Fiona. Fiona married her farmer and they have three children." I was speechless! He was laughing, watching the astonished expression cross my face. When I finally got over the surprise I asked Bill, "The next time you see Fiona, ask her if she remembers?"

Tinputz, Bougainville Island

The Trip of a Lifetime

From 1971 to 1973 my husband and I lived at Tinputz on Bougainville Island. John was the only teacher at Tinputz Vocational Centre with an enrolment of approximately twenty students. Our eldest son Andrew was just two years old. We had two more children while living there, both of whom were born at St Mary's, Vunapope Mission, Kokopo, East New Britain. Melanie was born in 1971 and Dylan in 1973.

Tinputz was my first experience of travelling overseas and living in an isolated area. At the time, if I had known what the conditions were like, I may well have reneged, but my only thoughts were, this is going to be a really big adventure! And so it was!

Living isolated taught me so much about myself. It demonstrated that the simple things in life are best. John departed for Tinputz first and approximately three weeks later, Andrew and I left Australia. I only carried luggage that I could manage, which consisted of clothing and the barest of necessities for Andrew and myself. When our cargo did arrive, three months later, I was hugely embarrassed at the amount of paraphernalia. Once sorted, we repacked two-thirds of the crate and sent it home.

Within that three-month hiatus, I had learned to grate fresh coconut using a shell and gently dry it out in the oven. Fresh coconut milk was used as stock in casseroles, and a colander was utilised as a sieve when making bread or baking cakes. Food orders were initially hard to obtain and had to come by sea from Rabaul, so we lived off the trees and out of the trade store, coupled at times with neighbourly hospitality. There was no electricity, so two kerosene lanterns were hung from the low-slung lounge room ceiling of a night-time. Having sweated in the humidity all day, the heat from the lamps pulsated downwards which kept the sweat rolling down our backs. Flying foxes *(fockez)* enjoyed slaloms in and out the window struts and geckoes in all sizes and colours adorned the walls, playing chasey. There were two kerosene fridges that rarely worked. A slow combustion stove and a two-burner primus were my other *headaches!* Like kneading bread, life on Bougainville slowly began to mould itself into shape.

Owing to the poor condition of the Vocational Centre, John was running around in ever-increasing circles due to the lack of tools and insufficient funds. He was so angry at the disinterest in the school's plight, he wrote to the Education Department stating that if the school didn't receive some supportive attention, the Vocational Centre would soon be without a manager. Unbeknown to us at the time, the previous manager had left the school A$1,000 in debt. The school, we learned, was responsible for its own economic viability.

This galvanised John into action. The Education Department supplied tinned fish and rice for the students, so to supplement this meagre diet the boys cleared and prepared gardens to grow kau kau (sweet potato) and green vegetables. They added fresh fish to their diet when they could, with any surplus fish being sold to the local villages. John and the boys also built a small trade store, much to the chagrin of the local trade store owner, but John was keen to give the boys as broad an education as possible. Next to the trade store a rough-hewn oven, similar to today's outdoor pizza ovens, was also built. It smoked from every orifice but worked a treat.

My role was to teach the boys how to make bread rolls. These were sold at their trade store and turned out to be a great success. John also bought three young sows and a boar from one of the local plantations in the hope the pigs would produce offspring, thereby availing the school of more income. Slowly but surely funds began to trickle in. A large coconut and cocoa plantation was attached to the school so the boys built a smoke-house (haus smok), for copra drying. They also sold the wet cocoa bean when it was harvested. These activities took a great deal of time but bonded the boys together with the incentive of learning new skills and making the school a viable entity.

The school itself was seriously run-down and a lot of work was required for it to become fully operational. The dormitories needed major repairs and the cooking facilities for the students had to be rebuilt. Unfortunately, after a monsoonal rain, torrents of water spilling out of the mountains flooded the Irung River behind the school, resulting in the mess, which was located on the river bank, being washed out to sea.

While the school seemed to lurch from one disaster to another, the upside was the boys were learning how to build and repair structures as well as plumbing skills. Over time, the local Mission and some villages down the coast requested the boys build concrete bases for installing water tanks, which were paying jobs. John also managed to secure an Administration Toyota, which was being written off. John rode his motorbike to Buka. On his return, he was loaded down with the bike in the back and several natives who variously hitched a ride when a vehicle was available. Owing to the heavy rains at the time, the tracks were mud-coated and the Toyota skidded off the road and slid down a steep embankment, which left John having to walk home. There was no way he could retrieve the vehicle or the bike. Word spread about the dilemma, and a plantation manager came to the rescue. He and his sixty Chimbu (local) workers took a long, strong, thick length of rope and they pulled the Toyota up the steep, slippery slope and back on to the track. It was a mighty effort! We were so grateful!

When the Toyota finally arrived, nothing gave the boys greater pleasure than to hang over the motor while John explained all the parts and taught them how to take bits apart and clean them etc. The Toyota was a bit of a *bomb*, but it gave us, as a family, a set of wheels and a lot more mobile freedom. Being so old, the vehicle did have its moments!

***

On ninth April 2019 John and I, and our three grown-up children travelled back to PNG. Tinputz has always been held very close to our hearts and as John and I are getting older we wanted to visit again while we were still able. Mel had completed Kokoda three years earlier and was keen to see other parts of PNG. Andrew held only faint memories of Tinputz.

We first visited St Mary's, Vunapope, to show Mel and Dylan where they were born. Matron very kindly showed us around. I found it to be a very emotional experience. When I walked through the hospital doors, I was quite overcome with memories. Tears spilled. The hospital hadn't changed in forty-five years.

In conversation with two Indigenous nurses in the corridor, one of them said, "So when you were here many years ago, you were young and pretty."

I gave an odd smile and replied, "Mmm, maybe, but now I'm old and wrinkly."

The nurse responded, "Yes, you are!"

I cried laughing! I just love native naiveté.

Two days later we flew to Buka and were transported back to Tinputz thanks to Bosco from *Bougainville Experience Tours*. The

Vocational Centre no longer exists but the Bougainville Technical College, Tinputz, has taken its place. The College caters for up to 300 students. It is a co-ed boarding school teaching Trades as well as Media and Hospitality. The Principal of the College, John, welcomed us, as did the Shire President, whose father had been Shire President when we lived in Tinputz. We met several of the teachers and some of the students who welcomed us with a very tasty lunch. Thanks to Noella, the Media Teacher, who took some videos of us, and is hopefully putting together some history of Tinputz from the photos and information we have since supplied.

After lunch we explored the area, which has changed so much since our time. When we lived at Tinputz, there were six European-type houses and Tsicot Village. The coconut and cocoa plantations are no longer there, but Tinputz has approximately fifty new-looking homes. We visited our old house, which was still standing. It has been converted into a duplex, housing two of the College teachers. The house was originally built in the 1950s and was home to the then Assistant District Commissioner. I was hopeful that revisiting Tinputz, Andrew might have some flashbacks, even though he was very young at the time. When we walked to the front of the house, which faces the sea, he could remember running down the small slope towards the beach.

Prior to our trip I had contacted Bosco, asking him if he could put the word out that John Reeves was returning to Tinputz in the hope that some of John's ex-students might be able to meet up with us. In Bosco's vehicle, we crossed the bridge at the Irung River and alighted on the southern side. Andrew's big toe had been cut off at this river when his foot slipped between the chain and the sprocket of a motorbike, in 1973. We thought we might see if we could find the toe!

***

The Japanese, in recompense for WWII atrocities, are building bridges from Buka to Buin on Bougainville, across the multitudinous rivers that cascade down from the mountains,. The bridges are most welcome as some of the rivers were and still are treacherous crossings. While standing at the Irung, we were so excited to meet up with Tomas Khabis, one of John's ex-students. So many funny and wonderful memories came flooding back. Tomas was so excited to see John. He couldn't stop hugging him! Tomas is now headman of his village and has fifteen grandchildren.

***

That night we stayed at the Tinputz Mission, with many thanks to Father Robert and Sylvia, and the lovely ladies who so very kindly looked after us. Sylvia was a little girl when we lived at Tinputz and she remembered us. That night we were serenaded in our beds by beautiful hymn singing practice, coming from the Tinputz church, for Palm Sunday.

The following day we travelled to Arawa and caught a motorised canoe to Pok Pok Island, which is just the most beautiful, peaceful retreat. The memory of pristine blue water; gentle waves lapping; chatting with the locals; the casual, laid-back lifestyle; the shy piccaninnies giggling and laughing when spoken to; the gorgeous smiles returned; Dylan paddling in an outrigger with a young boy; Mel paddleboarding; the sound of silence. Just magic!

***

We took seven flights in eight days. Yes, it was a 'flying' visit but owing to other commitments, this was all we could manage. One flight was cancelled, which saw us relaxing and enjoying the beautiful Rapopo Resort outside Kokopo. Fortunately it did little to delay our itinerary.

One of the most endearing memories of revisiting PNG is the welcome we received by many of the locals. The Tolai were so excited to know that Mel and Dylan were 'one of them!' People, in general, were curious to know why we were there, more particularly because we, as a family, look alike. They were so very grateful to learn that we had lived on Bougainville and shared some of their experiences, and that we had returned after all these years and not forgotten them. Our trip was so enlightening, educational and fun in reminiscence, there is no way we would or could ever forget! It was the trip of a lifetime!

***

The following was written by John Reeves:

Memories – come flooding back;

The smell of smoke drifting lazily from the copra house, the sweet smell of wet cocoa bean;

The scent of rain forest, tropical fruit, flowers, the sea, the air after rain;

The muffled sound of waves breaking on the outer reef – constant, calming, reliable;

The rapid fall of sunset brings the sounds of the night; sounds that set the place, set the time, set the feeling;

The sight of kids playing on the beach with shells, sticks, imagination and enthusiasm;

The gentle slap of waves against the prow of a fishing canoe;

The sounds of laughter amid a distant conversation drifting across the still waters of the bay;

Raucous screams of delight from excited teenagers packed precariously on the back of a truck carefully negotiating a fast-flowing stream;

The beautiful harmony of island voices preparing for the Palm Sunday service;

The soft warmth of a morning greeting, the rapid-fire chaos of pidgin English – taking you from a degree of puzzled understanding to a place of total confusion;

Dappled light on a jungle trail; coconut trees so much taller than before;

The pride of well-kept gardens and village surrounds;

Waking to the sound of a bomb casing being struck marking the start of a new day;

Barking geckos patrolling the walls and ceiling; lights that flicker, die and reappear as the clapped-out generator struggles against demand overload;

The women carrying piccaninnies and possessions in a hand-woven string bag; the men, proud, dark glasses, bare feet, torn T-shirt and a bush knife;

Chooks, dogs, pigs and kids galore; so many kids, bleached hair, shy with sunny smiles;

Groups of people standing by the road waiting for a Public Motor Bus to pick them up for a bone-shaking journey to Buka;

The dedication of nurses and teachers in the woefully under-resourced medical centres and schools;

The great joy of meeting Tomas again, recalling the time when he was a quiet, shy student at the Vocational Centre and is now the headman of his village, with the responsibility to care for thousands of acres of bush running from the mountain foothills to the beach;

Navy bread for breakfast – 4 x 4 inches of edible particle board with a taste to match; a stubby of S.P.Green, most welcome at the end of the day;

Pausing on the bank of the fast-flowing Ramazon River and wondering how I ever rode through the waist-deep water on the little yellow Honda;

Realising that foreign aid really does make a difference; a bridge, an all-weather road, a new classroom, a mobile phone tower; Lives changed for the better.

Oh To Be in England

After retirement, I was to travel to England with an old school friend, from Melbourne. We planned to hire a car and drive to Cornwall with the intention of visiting all over the area. Unfortunately my friend suffered a serious heart attack eight weeks prior to departure. This left me in a huge quandary. I had never travelled overseas on my own and was quaking at the thought. Everything had been booked and paid for. What to do?

A friend strongly encouraged me to make the trip, offering advice on the how/what/where and whys of travelling alone. The gut-wrenching fear and trepidation was palpable but I duly arrived in London and spent three full days seeing the sights. I then picked up a vehicle at Heathrow Airport and headed south, spending that night in Dover. Suffice to say the nerve ends were stretched to the max! I didn't understand the hi-tech GPS and the car company representative walked off before showing me how to find reverse.

Wanting to see the white cliffs, I woke early the following morning and headed in their direction. Unused to the congestion of English traffic and trying to drive and 'spot' at the same time, I suddenly found myself following a semitrailer, hemmed in by a line of witch's hats. The semi and I ended up in a very large open area with no checkpoints and the semi then magically disappeared. Where was I?

To cut a long story short, and yes, you guessed it, I was in the ferry terminal to France. An Indian gentleman, with the strongest English accent of anyone I met on that month-long trip, was trying to literally push me on to the ferry. Many tears and with much shaking of fists and swearing by both parties, he explained seven things not to do and two things to do, regarding exiting the terminal. Doh! Like I was going to remember all these jumbled-up instructions? Taking off, I did a complete circuit according to what I understood and ended up back in the queue. More tears and more shaking of fists as someone else also tried to push me towards the ferry. Much to my chagrin, I finally managed to find the exit ('just follow the Owls,' – cartoon pics – they said!) and eventually found my way down the steepest, scariest hairpin-bend road ever, to the cliffs. When I finally reached the stony beach, I stumbled out of the car, shaking. My nerves were frayed.

How was I ever going to drive myself around England for a month, if every day was like this? Surveying the scene, I waddled on wooden legs along the stony beach, taking note of the old rusted remains from WWII and trying to focus on what I had actually come to see. Realising how thirsty I was, I returned to the car for a drink. No-one else was around, probably because it was so early, and Mother Nature was calling. Checking the surrounds, I scurried along the stony beach towards a grass-cropped headland and let go with a loud, relieved sigh!

In relaying the full story to some English people in Cornwall a few days later, they all laughed hysterically and said, "Noreen, you should have gotten on the ferry, you'd have had a wonderful view of the cliffs from there!"

That first week in England was a heart starter. I was totally unprepared for the volume of traffic and the number of people. Being used to wide-open spaces it took some time to come to terms with the cramped, narrow roads, speed signs in mph and the constant stop-start traffic. On contemplation, and determined to drive around England, I hung on to Lao Zhu's philosophy – 'The journey of a thousand miles begins with a single step' – I had to remind myself of this on a daily basis!

After zigzagging north from Dover via Sissinghurst's beautiful gardens, down to Lewes and Brighton, then off to Winchester and Salisbury, I hit the coast again near Litton Cheney, which is one of the most charming small villages I have ever seen. It took my breath away. I stayed in the Youth Hostel there and had dinner at a very friendly pub.

As I was keen to keep moving, the following day I passed through Lyme Regis and enjoyed walking around the old battlement-type structures that were part of the old port. The history here had me spellbound. I remember placing my hands on the rough-hewn bluestone walls near the water's edge, wanting to absorb a taste of the reality of the people who built these structures that held back the sea; to feel what they felt; see what they saw. One could only imagine! In the thirteenth century, it was a major British port and is historically known for its fossils.

Being an ex-Victorian, Torquay was next on my list, and this is where the trip suddenly went pear-shaped. Somehow I missed the turnoff and ended up lost – in Paignton. There were so many narrow, winding streets I became completely bamboozled and ended up going the wrong way up one-way streets or else driving around in circles. I eventually found a small service station and pulled in, in the hope of receiving directions. Map in hand, I entered the tiny office. Three elderly local gentlemen greeted me, and the fun began!

Explaining my dilemma, the following unfolded. I will call these three gentlemen Ned, Ted and Fred, for the sake of the story, and please keep in mind, if you have ever watched *The Vicar of Dibley*, they were the epitome of *Jim Trott*, played brilliantly by Trevor Peacock. I will be so bold as to say I think Trevor must have modelled the *Jim Trott* character on these three.

Me: Good afternoon gentlemen. I'm an Aussie and I'm lost. Can you please help me find my way out of Paignton. I'm looking for a particular highway (number provided) but keep driving around in circles.

Dead silence. They all looked at each other.

Ned: "Well, well, ahh, mmm, what do you think Ted?"

Ted: Looking around for assistance. "Ahh. Um. Well, I dunno." Hesitation. "Do you know, Fred?"

Fred: "Mmm. Well, where is it exactly that you want to go again? Mmm. I think you should turn around, drive to the end of this street, and turn right."

The three men then began a discussion on this way, that way or the other way with none of them in agreement as to which way was best.

Me: "But there is no turn right. I've just come from there and it was a left-hand turn only."

Fred: "No, no, no, no, no. Just go up to the end and turn right. That should put you back on the main road."

I looked at the three in total confusion. I knew there was no right turn but did not wish to openly contradict him again.

Me: "Can you tell me where this road goes if I drive straight ahead?"

Ned: "Oh, I don't know where that road goes. I never been down there. Lived 'ere all me life but I never been down that road."

Me: "Have either of you other two gentlemen been down that road?"

Fred and Ted together: "No, no, no we don't use that road. We don't know where it goes."

I was baffled.

Me: "So what about one of these side roads out here?"

Ned: "Oh, no, no, no, no, no. Yes, they're no good. There's nuthin' down there. You won't get out that way."

Me: "Right. So you don't recommend straight ahead.

Fred: "No, no, no."

Unfolding the map once more, I pointed to the highway I wanted to find and asked them to point on the map where we currently were. That didn't work. They didn't know how to read the map. Approximately twenty minutes had passed since I'd entered the office and I was beginning to feel extremely frustrated, partially owing to the quite long silences that fell between the questions and answers. Unfortunately there was a noticeable shortage of passing people. I felt completely isolated.

Finally, Fred spoke up again. "Just turn around and drive to the end of the street where I said and you'll see the right-hand turn. I've lived here all me life. There is a right-hand turn up that end.

I smiled and pointed, "That end?"

Fred: "Yes, that's right!"

I thanked the three gentlemen for their efforts and bade them farewell. I turned the car around with grave misgivings and drove to the end of the street, as directed. There was no right-hand turn! Retracing my steps, I passed the service station and drove straight ahead. Following the road around to the right I discovered the beach with hundreds of beautiful, brightly coloured bathing boxes. Unfortunately there was no photo opportunity because there was nowhere to park. Continuing on at a very slow pace I carefully wound my way through the town by sticking to the outskirts, found a right-hand turn that looked promising and eventually discovered the required highway.

After the first week of being more lost than found and having seen places I knew I would never find again, I began to settle into the trip, visiting beautiful Devon and Sussex (England's best kept secret), up to Gloucester, down to Bristol on the train, through the Cotswolds to Oxford and Stratford-upon-Avon, north to the gorgeous Peak District, tackling roundabouts within roundabouts that completely did my head in, across to Lancashire (the county that is smaller than our sheep station), north to the Lake District, through the stunning, isolated Yorkshire Dales to Whitby, Scarborough and historic, beautiful York, finishing in Cambridge.

Cambridge was my last stop before attempting the harrowing journey to return the car to Heathrow. I remember feeling totally daunted at this prospect. Having driven around England for a month, the date was looming and I was in panic mode. Fear gripped me for the three days prior. Attempting to stay focused was difficult. I had the GPS code but the 'what-ifs' popped up like popcorn bursting out of a hot pan. What-if this? What-if that? They even popped up in my manic dreams.

Day two before delivery, my inner self worked at clamping down the fear and the self-talk kicked in. Breathe. Take your time. Relax. Take a break when you need it. Drink water. Eat an apple. Take a short walk. Go to the toilet. Just go with the flow, drive carefully and listen to the GPS instructions.

'D' day arrived. I listened to my inner self even though I could feel the blood pumping through my ears. The day was misty damp and the traffic was heavy, but manageable. Two hours later, I was heading into Heathrow, recognising some familiar roads. *Siri* finally announced, 'you have arrived at your destination.' With 2,058 miles under my belt, I got out and kissed the ground.

The Reluctant Clown

A challenging writing group exercise that began with us drawing two pieces of paper from a hat. Each had an occupation on it and we were allowed to choose which to write about. I got taxi driver and clown. I considered combining them as I have known a few taxi drivers who were right clowns, but in the end I went with this. I hope you enjoy it.

Reggie Downer was a humble young man who never quite seemed to shine, for want of a better word, in his or anyone else's opinion. Reggie was one of those kids who scraped through school, just passing the basics with no great scholarly skills. He was twenty-two years old and the sixth of twelve children. The family was almost destitute. His parents eked out a meagre living from the poor, stony tor their house was perched on and the few gravelly paddocks they owned. A mottled stand of stringy barks stood many metres from the house, which afforded little shelter from the cold winter winds and no shade from the hot summer sun. They grew vegetables and ran a few scraggy sheep that kept them in meat on occasions, and a clutch of hens provided some small relief to their basic diet. Every evening his mum would sit and spin the harsh, hairy wool that the scrawny sheep reluctantly gave up – the gentle treadle and soft hum of the spinning wheel being a form of calm meditation after a hard day outside.

Their small, humble home was a blend of second-hand timber and corrugated iron, bound together with whatever fixtures could be scrounged. It consisted of a large kitchen that housed an Aga combustion stove rescued from the local tip. Three bedrooms meant the kids had to top and tail when they slept. Some of the older siblings worked night shifts, allowing them to sleep through the day while the younger children were at school. Outside, the toasty aroma of chopped wood emanated from a ramshackle woodshed, which leaned precariously against its neighbour, the outhouse.

The kids had to make their own way as there was little incentive shown regarding making a go of it in life. Reggie's parents were both illiterate and with such a large litter of kids, just keeping food on the table and clothes on their backs occupied their every waking hour. Although life was hard, his parents did the best they could for their large brood. Collectively, they accepted their lot in life and made the most of what little they had.

***

Reggie was an unusual looking lad, what they call pear-shaped, with bony shoulders angling out to rotund hips and thighs. His turquoise blue eyes that were his redeeming feature were constantly under threat from a thick, mousey-coloured fringe. He was ungainly at best and the kids at school mercilessly teased him. He was hopeless at sports but Reggie was used to the jokes and took the teasing in his stride.

Having completed Year 9, Reggie left school and found odd jobs wherever he could, contributing his sometimes meagre salary to the household. He was a soft, affable soul and although he lacked ambition, he was happy to help provide for the family in any way he could. Nothing was ever too much trouble; he was always willing to help out. In the process, he managed to pick up a few trade skills here and there, sometimes with supervisors taking him under their wing, sympathetic to his situation. He never complained and took on every task he was required to do, whether he knew how to do it or not. His gentle nature and ready smile endeared him to many of his co-workers. His soft side made him an easy target for the rougher men, but he took their jibes and insults with good grace.

***

A circus came to town, which caused great excitement among the local community. As there was little entertainment on offer, Reggie decided to treat himself. Wandering around the animal enclosures, the elephants and lions had him captivated. He wasn't too fond of the disdainful looking camels and gave them a wide berth, but the cheeky monkeys had him in fits of laughter with their comical antics. They made him feel like a little kid again. He stood for a while watching a couple of trainers lunging one of the horses. He loved these beautiful, intelligent animals. How he wished he could ride!

Scouting around the trailers and cages behind the Big Top, Reggie noticed one of the horse handlers having difficulty controlling a large white gelding outside the stables. The horse was wild-eyed and rearing. The handler, whose face bore the visage of a painted clown, was giving the horse a taste of the whip. The horse reared again, then bucked, sending the handler flying and losing control of the reins. Two more bucks and the horse headed straight for Reggie. Innocently, he stood his ground. With his head down, the horse ran and looked as though he was going to run over the top of Reggie, but to everyone's amazement, Reggie held up his hand as the animal approached. The horse slid to a gravelly stop. They looked at each other, the horse whinnying and tossing its head and magnificent mane in defiance, allowing Reggie to grab the reins as they flicked past. Holding them close he murmured, "There, there boy, it's ok. Take it easy." The horse snorted but stood still, pawing one foreleg into the gravel. Reggie gave him a rub on the nose then quietly patted the animal's neck, crooning to him softly.

The handler, having picked himself up, raced over to where the pair was standing. As he went to grab the reins the horse pulled back again, hard. Reggie eyed the handler suspiciously. "It's alright," he said, a deep frown furrowing his brow, "just tell me where you want me to take him and I'll bring him right along." With an angry look the handler growled, "Follow me." Reggie led the horse away at a slow trot. Unbeknown to both men the Ringmaster had been watching the whole process. Once the gelding was back in his stall, Reggie gave him a final pat. The big horse rubbed his head up and down Reggie's shirt and attempted to nibble his ear.

"Hey," Reggie yelled as he giggled and pulled away from the animal. "My ear isn't a meal! He's a beautiful animal," Reggie remarked, looking over his shoulder at the handler, who, in turn, gave Reggie a filthy look and swore under his breath.

"He needs a good thrashing," the handler said, "and I was just about to give him one when you showed up." Reggie looked at the handler in astonishment as the Ringmaster strode into the stable carrying a small riding crop, with a look that matched thunder.

"I heard that," said the Ringmaster, "and I think from now on this young man might be in charge of Hunter, if he happens to be looking for a job. As for you Mr Knight, I've told you before, Hunter needs a firm hand, not the whip, yet you continue to take no notice of my directions and abuse him. You only make him worse. Take yourself to the Paymaster and collect your dues, then pack your bags and get out. We don't need your kind around here! We'll find another clown, even if it means going without one for a while."

Turning his back to Knight, the Ringmaster spoke to Reggie, "You have a definite knack young man. Where did you learn your horse skills?"

Reggie stood there blinking, his mouth wide open.

"C'mon man, speak up."

"I didn't know I had any horse skills, sir," Reggie almost whispered.

The Ringmaster gave a loud guffaw.

"You didn't know you had any horse skills eh! Well my friend, there aren't too many people I know who can halt a large gelding running straight at them. You must have some skill to stop an animal like that."

"A-a-ll I did was hold up my hand," Reggie stammered.

"Hah!" the Ringmaster roared, "show me your hand."

Reggie held up his hand in a stop sign.

The Ringmaster couldn't stop laughing. "Come with me."

Reggie followed the Ringmaster around the back of the stables to where the staff caravans were parked. He was wide-eyed in wonder at the size of them. At the far end, a six-wheel maroon-coloured van was parked, covered in gold scrawls and swirls that were splayed across its length. The Ringmaster opened the door and motioned Reggie to enter. An audible gasp escaped his lips as he stepped inside. He thought he had entered a palace and stood there, rooted to the spot.

"Move in mate," said the Ringmaster, "I can't get past."

Reggie took two more small steps as the tall man pushed past him, ducking his head a little as he entered.

"Sit down! Take the weight off."

Reggie looked at the plush velvet-covered seats and unwittingly brushed his backside.

"Well then," said the Ringmaster, as he leaned against the stove with his arms crossed, "What's your name son?"

"Reggie."

"Well Reggie, my name is Sam Treloar, but everyone calls me Mr Treloar or Ringmaster. Your choice! I don't mind which."

"Thank you," said Reggie, in a small voice.

Treloar gave Reggie a broad, toothy smile as creases flared out from the corners of his dark-brown eyes and disappeared into the lines on his strong, tanned face.

"Would you like a cup of tea Reggie?"

"Yes please, with milk, if that's ok?" was all Reggie could manage. His gaze wandered around the interior in total wonderment. He never knew mobile homes could look like this.

As Treloar placed the kettle on the stove he quietly observed Reggie studying the kitchenette – the two stainless steel sinks, the fridges, the TV above the table and the shiny timber cupboards. Midnight blue velvet curtains loosely framed every window. A multitude of crystal glasses sparkled behind the glass-covered cupboard doors overhead. Reggie sat there spellbound. He had entered another world.

Treloar was no fool. His avuncular nature understood who he was looking at and admired the lad for his naiveté and obvious innocence. Placing a mug of steaming tea in front of Reggie, Treloar sat down opposite and asked him if he would like to join the circus.

"Join the circus?" Reggie stammered. He couldn't believe his ears!

"Strike me lucky, Mr Treloar, I'd love to, but what could I do? I don't know nuthin' 'bout workin' in a circus." Treloar flashed his toothy grin again.

"That's ok Reggie, there's heaps to do and we could use another pair of capable hands around here. All the animals have to be fed twice a day, the horses have to be exercised, adjustments always have to be made to equipment and many of the performers need someone to hold apparatus for them while they practice their routines. We all lend a hand with whatever needs doing. We're like a big family. It's full on! You'll love it! And if you prove your worth, which I'm sure you will, the job will be a permanent one if you want it."

Reggie was speechless and smiled inwardly. He knew what a big family was, but to join the circus! Just think of it! His mind was in a whirl.

Hesitantly, Reggie replied, "I'd love to join, thank you, but I live a coupla k's outta town and …

Before he could finish the sentence, Treloar interrupted.

"You won't live at home son. You'll live here onsite, with all of us. We have singles accommodation and you can bunk in with some of the other blokes. They're a good bunch, mostly. Whaddaya say?"

Reggie's eyes moistened. "I'd love to Mr Treloar, thank you, but can I just run home and tell me Ma and Pa first?"

Treloar slapped himself on the knee and laughed heartily. "Of course you can. Welcome aboard!"

***

Reggie returned early the following morning. His parents were simple people and had misgivings about the offer as his monetary contribution to the family made a difference. Everyone knew the circus was not a permanent fixture. If Reggie remained employed, his assistance would be sorely missed once the circus moved on.

Downcast, Reggie reported to Treloar.

"Listen, young man, I completely understand where your parents are coming from, but there's no need to worry. We can set up a system whereby a nominated amount from your pay can be put aside each week. That money will be kept in the safe, here in my van and whenever you need to pass it on, you just have to let me know. How does that suit you?"

Reggie grinned. It suited him very well.

Shyness overcame him when Treloar walked him to the allotted caravan he was to share and introduced him to Stan, Jimmy and Jack, his room-mates. They seemed a congenial bunch and, after showing him where to stow his meagre possessions, went on to explain about the hours and routines they worked, some on shifts, others not and where the mess tent was for their grub.

"Why do they call it a mess?" Reggie asked.

They all looked at each other and burst out laughing.

"'Cos it usually is in a mess" Stan joked, then explained it was similar to a communal dining room. Reggie didn't know what a dining room was but was too shy to ask.

Work began at 6.00 am and the next week disappeared in a blur. Reggie had to feed the elephants and muck out their holding area. Then he had to feed the horses and muck out their stables, which was the best part for him. He loved the horsey smell and the aroma of fresh hay, even though it made him sneeze. He relished the work, and it showed. Many of the regular staff marvelled at how he was so willing and ready to learn, and how instinctive he was when it came to the animals. The best part of all was when he had to feed and clean out Hunter's stall. The big gelding wouldn't leave him alone and kept nuzzling his neck and back, all the while Reggie was laughing and telling the big *galoot*, as he called the horse, to stop tickling. The instant rapport between the horse and his new handler was not lost on Treloar, nor the entertainers who rode the horses in their acts.

Gizelle, the girl who mostly rode Hunter within the circus ring, took a shine to Reggie. She really appreciated his care and attention to the big horse. Yes, Hunter could be a handful at times, but with the right touch he could do just about anything that was asked of him. Gizelle asked Reggie if he would help her to teach Hunter how to bow. Reggie smiled. He was up for anything, especially if it involved Gizelle. She was petite, with thick, blonde curls that swirled all over her head. She always wore a black glove on her left arm which intrigued Reggie, but he was too polite to ask why. He thought it must be some quirky girly fashion thing. They set the training day for the next lay day of the circus, in two days time.

Late the following afternoon Reggie was cleaning out the elephant enclosure before breaking up the hay bales. The oppressive smell of warm dung hung in the air as the sun headed west in a brilliant, effervescent burst of orange glow. Intent on his task, out of the corner of his eye some movement caught his attention. Looking sideways, he thought he spotted a man dressed all in black, lurking around behind the Ringmaster's caravan. It was one of those moments when he wasn't sure whether he'd seen someone or imagined it, and just as Reggie doubted himself, the black clad figure moved again, keeping within the shadows of the vans.

Reggie threw the rake aside and hurried in that direction. Following the backs of the caravans, no-one was visible, but as he stepped out between two of them, Gizelle, Jack and Stan were questioning the man dressed in black.

"What's up? Why are you here?" Stan was saying, somewhat aggressively.

"Mind ya own business Mr Sticky Beak," was the reply.

"You shouldn't be here," said Gizelle.

"Oh, ya shouldn't be here," rebounded the sarcastic response in a forced, high-pitched voice. "I can be here if I want," the man snapped. "I came to collect some of me clobber I forgot the other day, so what's it to ya?"

"Listen Frank, this isn't a good idea," said Stan, trying to ease the tension. "If you forgot something why didn't you just go to the office or contact someone to let them know, instead of creeping around here late in the afternoon looking like you don't want to be seen. No-one's going to object if you need to collect your gear."

Reggie was standing on the periphery of the little group when Knight turned and saw him.

"Oh, my, my, my, if it isn't the little hero," snarled Knight. "Happy rescuing everything are we? Making a big hero of yaself! Thanks a million for getting me sacked!"

Stan took a decisive step forward. "Shut your mouth Knight. That was totally uncalled for. Treloar has spoken to you on a number of occasions about your treatment of the horses, especially Hunter. You've only got yourself to blame for your dismissal! It would be a very good idea if you collect whatever it is and get out!"

"Mind ya own damn business and naff off, the lotta ya," the man sneered angrily, and stubbing out his cigarette, he stormed off.

"Who was that?" Reggie asked, as Gizelle, Stan and Jack stood there, looking slightly bewildered, their gaze following the retreating figure.

"Mmm," said Stan, "that was Frank Knight, the Clown that was sacked recently. The bloke that was whipping Hunter just before you came along."

"Oh, him! He didn't sound like a very nice person. He was very rude to all of you!"

Gizelle couldn't resist a quiet smile.

"Yes Reggie," she said. "Frank could be a nasty piece of work when he wanted. We were all a little afraid of him, at times."

Starting early the following morning, Reggie fed Hunter before he led him into the Big Top. Gizelle felt it was better to train him there because that was where Hunter mostly performed. She indicated to Reggie what she required and the training began. With Gizelle's direction and Reggie's patience, the horse learned quickly. One hour into the lesson they heard a commotion outside. People were running everywhere, yelling. Gizelle hurriedly led Hunter over to a large, square platform and, climbing up, she then jumped onto Hunter's back.

"Hurry Reggie," she yelled. "Quick, jump up, something weird is happening outside."

Reggie quaked. He'd never ridden a horse before.

"Reggie. Quick!"

As he clambered onto the platform he stammered, "Gizelle, I've never ridden a horse."

"Oh, don't be such a goose. There's nothing to it! Just get on and hang on!"

The minute Reggie was seated, Hunter took off with Reggie stifling a yelp into a mouth full of golden curls. Gizelle caught his right hand and wrapped it around her waist as they cantered out of the ring. Reggie hung on to her for dear life before he realised he could wrap his other arm around her also. His face was scarlet. He wasn't quite sure where to put his hands. He felt embarrassed but loved the smooth glide of the horse under him and the mouth full of soft curls. He couldn't remember ever feeling so exhilarated.

They cantered over to where most of the circus employees were gathered, outside Treloar's caravan. A police car was parked at the scene, its flashing red and blue lights still circling on the vehicle's roof. Gizelle dropped the reins and, sliding off Hunter, she pushed her way through the crowd leaving Reggie sitting on the horse, paralysed in fear. Now what? Hunter stood there patiently as Reggie eventually leant forward on to his stomach and managed to slide his right leg over the horse's rump. He slipped to the ground with his face pressed against Hunter's warm flank. He couldn't believe what had happened. He'd just ridden a horse with his arms wrapped around the most exciting girl in the world. His mouth was so dry all he could think of was that he wanted a drink of water.

Hanging at the back of the crowd, Reggie couldn't see or hear what caused the commotion. He was about to walk away when the Ringmaster strode towards him accompanied by a police sergeant. A grim look twisted Treloar's visage.

On seeing Reggie, a thin, tight-lipped smile spread across his face.

"Ah, Reggie, just the man I'm looking for!"

"Yes Mr Treloar, what's happening? Can I do anything to help?"

"That's my man," said Treloar, slapping Reggie on his back, "I have a new job for you. Come with me." The buzz from the employees outside Treloar's caravan was audible as Treloar and the Sergeant strode off towards the Circus Office, with Reggie in hot pursuit.

"The thing is, Reggie, I have two problems. Hopefully the Sergeant here is going to help me with the first one and ideally you're going to help me with the second. I was exercising that young colt early this morning, you know, the one I bought last week, and the damn horse threw me. Once I'd caught the animal, I returned to my caravan only to find the door had been jimmied open and my safe robbed. The small box I keep the money in has been stolen, which includes your contributions to your mum and dad. But before you get upset I want to assure you — you won't be out of pocket. I will cover that sum for you. Now, only two employees knew where my safe was hidden and I have supplied the Sergeant with their names.

A puzzled look crossed Reggie's face.

"I'm very sorry to hear this Mr Treloar, but what's all this got to do with me?"

"Aha, I'm glad you asked Reggie. As you are well aware, our Circus Clown, Frank Knight, was sacked last week and the circus is suffering because clowns are an integral part of any performance. Because of your placid nature and willingness to help out in just about everything, I've decided to offer you the circus clown job. Whaddaya reckon?"

Reggie sat there stupefied. Disbelieving.

"I c-c-an't take Mr Knight's place Mr Treloar. I don't know nuthin' 'bout bein' a clown!"

"Aw, c'mon Reggie, there's nothing to it. The girls will dress you up and paint your face and you can go out there and entertain the spectators. You've seen Knight perform a few times. Just do what he did."

Reggie's mouth drooped. He could hear blood pumping through his ears. His heart hammered.

"Mr Treloar," he gasped, "please don't ask me to do this. I love my job. I don't want to lose it, but I can't do this. I'm not a performer."

"Nonsense Reggie. The reason I'm asking you is because of who you are. You haven't recognised it yet, but you have something many people don't possess. You have compassion towards your fellow man and everyone and everything you come in contact with. You may not be a *performer*, as you say, but your inner light shines and it's what everyone sees."

"Well thanks Mr Treloar but they ain't gunna see it through padding, funny clothes and face paint," said Reggie indignantly.

Treloar smiled.

"That's just it mate! You can't hide behind face paint. People will see you for who you are, no matter what!"

Reggie cringed.

'Please Mr Treloar, I can't! I'm already scared stiff thinkin' 'bout your suggestion!"

Treloar sat back with his arms folded. He turned his gaze to the Sergeant and gave him a quick, sly wink.

"You know something Reggie, life is a test and sometimes good things come our way and sometimes the not-so-good. I think you've seen quite a bit of the latter in your time. I'm asking you to take up this challenge because I believe you have it in you, to show more of your true self than just mucking out stables and feeding elephants. You just have to give yourself a bit of a boost now and again, when something falls in your lap."

"Yeah! Well I know whose lap I'm gunna fall in! Me own! In a big fat, splashy puddle. I'll make a complete fool o' meself."

Treloar grinned.

"Well, isn't that what clowning is all about?"

A sigh emptied from deep within. "Aw, Mr Treloar, I'm beggin' ya, please don't do this to me. I'd rather you asked me to split the atom!" Saying this, Reggie stood. He'd had enough of this conversation, but just as he reached the office door he turned slowly and looked at the two men, a frown creasing his brow.

"What's up?" asked Treloar.

Reggie hesitated. "I'm truly sorry to hear about the robbery but I've just remembered something. Frank Knight was here yesterday afternoon. Gizelle, Stan and Jack were talking to him. I saw and heard them. Knight got quite nasty. Thought ya might like to know!"

The Sergeant and Treloar stared at Reggie in amazement.

"Reggie," spluttered Treloar, "you are one son of a gun!"

***

The following day dawned with the sun marbling the sky as it hatched from behind the last of a silky night cloud. The pungent aroma of elephant dung mingled with the herbal undertone of musky earth, the elephant *cakes* looking like large steam puddings fresh out of the oven. Fat shadows fanned out into filigree fingers as they stretched across the dewy paddocks, waning as the sun climbed higher into a clear blue sky, wrapping the earth in a tingly freshness. Birds stirred each other with their early morning wake-up calls. Cattle lowed in the distance. The day was coming alive.

Reggie surfaced to a hive of activity but his subterranean emotions kept him under the covers. Normally he would bound out of bed, eager to begin the day, but this morning his sluggish emotions were a bulwark against making the first move. He had never felt real fear before and he struggled to understand the grind that was keeping him paralysed.

"Hurry up Reggie," Jack yelled. "You haven't had your breakfast and you'll be late. We can't be late today! We've got two shows to get through. Move it!"

Reggie reluctantly threw the covers off and dragged himself over the side of the bunk. His legs felt wooden.

Swerving from one emotion to another, Reggie skipped breakfast and embroiled himself in his work. Cindy, the oldest elephant, seemed particularly interested in Reggie this morning and although her food had been delivered, she kept poking Reggie with her trunk, at one point almost tipping him over as he bent to break up a hay bale.

"Hey Cindy, cut it out," he cried.

Cindy just stood there, gently swaying. She lightly tapped him on the shoulder. Reggie turned, and softened. "Sorry old girl," he said gently, giving her massive trunk a gentle pat. "I'm just not meself this morning." Cindy stopped her rocking and stared into Reggie's blue, bleary eyes. What passed between the elephant and her keeper, we will never know, but Reggie felt a little softer and a little better for her mute communication and understanding.

At 11:00 am Treloar and Gizelle found Reggie in the stables with the other workers.

"C'mon mate," said Treloar, barely able to conceal a cheeky grin, which was busting to erupt into something bigger. "Time to climb into your glad rags and slap on that smiley face!"

Reggie almost gagged as he clung to Hunter's mane.

"C'mon Reggie, you'll be fine!"

You could have heard a pin drop. Every hand in the stable was watching, and Reggie knew it.

Hunter gave a gentle whinny as Gizelle gently took Reggie by the elbow and, tugging him forward, told him all the girls were waiting, just dying to make him up. Reggie's legs almost went to water. Gizelle he could cope with but a room full of girls was another issue! Head down, he was led away like a shackled prisoner as loud wolf whistles and the banging of tin buckets could be heard in boisterous cacophony.

***

The Big Top was full to capacity. The hum of the crowd was like a thousand bee swarms filling the air with buzz and excitement. The acrobats, trapeze artists and jugglers were dressed in their multicoloured tights, all chattering and laughing, eagerly looking forward to their performances. The horses, decorated in their finery, jiggled and stamped on the spot, their bridles and martingales jingling and shining. The girls looked stunning seated on their mounts in their sequins and net, adorned with ostrich feathers on their heads in colours that matched their costumes, laughing and joking while they waited. Only one performer stood back from the others. Alone.

He felt a complete fool. He could feel the sweat soaking the padding wrapped around his waist. He was hot and incredibly uncomfortable. The yellow and black checked pants that hung from red braces made him feel like he was surrounded by a floppy parachute, which could possibly take off in a stiff breeze. The large black and white polka-dot bow tie kept slipping sideways and he had terrible trouble trying to walk in the oversized multicoloured shoes. He basically had to clump when he walked. But that wasn't the worst of it. The big spiky red wig made his head hot, causing it to itch uncontrollably and the make-up felt like he had thick cream plastered on his face. The red ball that was covering his nose was scratchy against his skin and he was scared he was going to cry. What if he did? The make-up would run and look twice as bad as it did now. His face twitched nervously, like horse haunches shooing flies. He was in a right pickle and all he wanted to do was run. Lilliputian like, Gizelle sat quietly, watching him from the line. She could see his distress but felt helpless to appease it. Gently, she nudged Hunter towards him, but Reggie saw them coming and turned away.

The performers quietly took their places behind Mr Treloar as the trumpets blared and the curtains opened in a flourish. The Ringmaster stepped forward in his top hat and tails, offset by tight cream jodhpurs and knee-length patent leather boots. He was an imposing sight! As he lead his team of entertainers around the ring the crowd erupted, clapping in time to the music as they marched. One of the jugglers grabbed Reggie around the neck and hauled him along just as the last of the performers were about to enter the ring. This act alone had the crowd in fits of laughter watching the clumpy clown being dragged along, totally unaware of the tumult that was camouflaged by baggy clothes and crazy make-up.

After several acts had the crowd tense with expectation and excitement, Reggie was literally pushed through the curtains by the Strong Man, almost tripping over his shoes as he propelled forward. Regaining his stature, he stood there, terrified, glued to the spot, wringing his hands. The scene ahead blurred. He felt like a blind person trying to decipher something alien. There was a collective split-second silence before everyone roared at the funny clown looking frightened. Reggie didn't know why they laughed and his fear escalated. The more angst he showed, the more the audience laughed. He knew he was supposed to move but his legs felt like they were set in cement. The bright lights dazzled him, the crowd terrified him. He was stage fright personified. From nowhere, a not so gentle nudge from Hunter shot him forward. He almost tripped again with the momentum while the crowd laughed and applauded his flailing arms and awkward gait. Reggie turned and saw Gizelle sitting astride the horse, smiling, giving him a gentle nod. The sight of her took his breath away.

Dressed all in white, Gizelle dazzled. Her close-knit net outfit hugged her slim frame, while the sequined bra top and bikini pants glittered and sparkled under the Big Top lights. Long white gloves covered her arms and soft white ostrich plumes shivered in the air every time she moved her head. Gizelle nodded at Reggie again as her eyes bored into his. She mouthed 'move!'

A strange feeling overcame Reggie as he stood there, visibly quaking. His thoughts flashed back to the look Cindy gave him in her enclosure this morning. The sight of Gizelle and Hunter standing there, exuding quiet encouragement, suddenly made his body feel light. He turned. Clumping along the side of the ring he spied a little girl, wide-eyed, watching him approach. She was eating fairy floss. Reggie stepped over the ring perimeter and approached her. Bending down, he held out his hand. The Big Top audience enfolded itself in silence. The little girl stared, then smiled and gave the Clown a high five. The crowd cheered! Taking the little girl gently by her sticky fingers he led her over to the ring and lifted her over the barrier. He signalled Gizelle to come forward and, in mime, indicated to the little girl would she like to ride the horse. Dropping her fairy floss in the sawdust, the little girl beamed and held up her arms to loud applause. Reggie placed the child in front of Gizelle who motioned Hunter forward. Spears of golden light bounced off the shining martingale as he pranced around the ring. When they returned, Gizelle gave Hunter a quiet command with her hands and feet. The big horse gave an exaggerated bow. The crowd went wild. The Clown beamed. Everything seemed to fall into place like money through a slot.

***

Gizelle was quietly congratulating Reggie at breakfast the following morning, but being so new to the role, Reggie's confidence wasn't exactly sky-high and he managed to convey this to Gizelle. She suggested they go to the Big Top and have a think about what could be implemented to pad out his *repertoire*, as she called it. Reggie had never heard that word before. He tried several times to say it to himself but his tongue couldn't quite wrap itself around the foreign word. The closest he came to pronouncing it was 'ratapa' and he knew that wasn't correct, so gladly gave up. He was learning so much he thought his head would explode with everything that was being crammed into it. He'd never ever had to think this hard, although he was secretly pleased with his performance, even though he thought his nerves would never stand the strain.

Once the think tank ideas had been agreed on, they proceeded to the mess for lunch. Finding Stan, Jack and Jimmy, they sat down beside them, feeling good about what they had decided. The three men gave them a sideways look, then got up and moved to another table. Gizelle and Reggie stared hard at each other, not understanding. Not being one to let something like this pass, Gizelle strode over to where the three men were sitting.

"What's going on here?" she asked. "Why did you look at us like that and get up and leave? What's the problem?"

Jimmy responded with a dirty look at Reggie. "Why don't you ask your little mate? He's full of surprises."

Gizelle stared. "Ask my little mate, WHAT? What do you mean he's full of surprises?"

"Ask him," said Stan in a very unfriendly tone."

"Look," said Gizelle, "if you've got something to say, say it! Neither of us understands what's got into the three of you. You were all ok at breakfast."

"Yeah, well we're not ok now," said Jimmy.

"Oh, for Pete's sake, spit it out!" Gizelle snapped.

Although Reggie had no idea what the problem was, hearing this exchange brought him to his feet. "There's obviously something very wrong here," he said, as he approached the table, "and neither Gizelle nor I know what it is. If it's about me then I would appreciate you telling us what it is."

The three blokes traded dark looks. With a deep sigh, Stan said, "Come with us."

Entering their shared accommodation, Reggie and Gizelle stood there, puzzled. They looked around, expecting to see something untoward, but couldn't decipher anything.

"So," said Gizelle, "what gives?"

The three men looked uncomfortable until Stan finally said, "Why don't you climb up and see what's sitting in your bunk, Clown," the last word being snapped out like a breaking twig.

Reggie and Gizelle looked at each other, uncomprehending.

Reggie slowly moved over to the bunk, looking at the others as he climbed up. A bulge showed under his blanket. Throwing the cover off, a small wooden box sat nestled into the mattress.

Reggie turned and looked at the three men. "What is this?" he asked, looking at them questioningly.

"You mean you don't know," proffered Jimmy.

"No, I don't know. I've never seen this box before. It doesn't belong to me!"

"We know it doesn't belong to you," said Stan, quite sarcastically.

"Then who does it belong to?" said Reggie, "and what's it doing in my bunk?"

"You tell us," said Stan.

Reggie stepped down, carrying the box with him. Placing it on the bench he opened the box and stared in astonishment. It was full of money.

Gizelle gasped! "Where did that come from?"

"It's Treloar's box that he keeps in his safe," said Stan.

"Hang on a minute," said Reggie, flabbergasted. "I didn't steal that box! How could I? Why would I steal it? It's got my own money in there that I put away for me mum and dad."

"We all know you come from a poor home," said Jimmy. "Maybe you thought a bit more dough would be a good thing."

"That's a lie," said Reggie defiantly. "I've never stolen anything in my life."

"Well, there's always a first time," sneered Jimmy.

"Just hold your horses right there," growled Gizelle. "You have no right to accuse Reggie of this. It's all supposition on your part. You've lived with and know what Reggie is like. How dare you accuse him without any proof."

The tension was tangible. You could have cut the atmosphere with a knife.

"Ok," said Reggie, after several tense minutes had passed, with them all scowling one way or another, "we'll call in Mr Treloar and see what he has to make of it."

Treloar knocked and entered the caravan. The sight that greeted him was a fraught, unhappy one, which disturbed him greatly. On his enquiring as to the issue, Stan took control and related the events of the morning. Jimmy, Stan and Jack had been sitting in the van prior to lunch, handballing a footy around to each other, laughing and joking. The footy had landed on Reggie's bunk and when Jimmy got up to retrieve it, that's when he discovered the box.

Treloar sat, thrumming his fingers on the small table, looking from one to the other of the five people before him. He loved and respected these guys and hated disharmony within his team. Jimmy looked angry; Jack was uncomfortable, fidgeting; Stan's arms were folded across his chest, his face unreadable. Gizelle was distraught, her eyes moist. Reggie just stood there, statue-like, his visage blank.

"Before I take this any further," said Treloar, "I want you to understand this. I do not believe for one minute that Reggie broke into my van and stole this money. For one thing, I doubt he would know how to jimmy a lock, let alone open a safe, particularly as he didn't even know where the safe was kept. There are only two other people who know where the safe is hidden in my van. One is Frank Knight, the other is Stan." At this, Stan started to remonstrate until Treloar held up his hand.

"It's ok Stan, I trust you implicitly so there's no cause for concern. I do know, however, that four of you saw Frank Knight here late yesterday, and there's one more thing! You three were with Reggie this morning in the stables around the time the robbery happened. If a certain person has been staking out the venue, then whoever it is knew I was exercising the colt and where you four were at the same time. We all pretty much know everyone's routines. It's not rocket science! So, my suggestion is this. I will call the police and they can come and take the box for fingerprint testing. The only prints on the box that should be found are my own, Frank Knight's, Jimmy's, and I believe Reggie's, as he lifted the box down from his bunk. If that's the case, it isn't too hard to assume who broke in and stole the box."

The afternoon dragged on. Stan, Jack and Jimmy made themselves scarce by keeping busy around the stables and staying out of the way. Everyone knew there had been strife, although many didn't understand why. No-one liked disharmony, especially before a performance, so people kept mostly to themselves. Reggie was at a loss. He didn't know where to put himself and he certainly didn't want to be in the van, so Gizelle shooed her room-mate out and invited him over to her accommodation. They sat together in silence. Despondency filled the air. The magic wand had been broken. Before Reggie left to feed the elephants, Gizelle asked him to wait. She went over the decisions they had made before lunch about what he was going to add to the evening's performance. They briefly ran through his *repertoire*, trying not to impinge too much on his troubled thoughts. Reggie just nodded, and left. His legs felt heavy. His heart even heavier.

***

The bustling, jostling, noisy spectators crowded into the Big Top just before 7.00 pm. The popcorn and fairy floss vendors were doing a roaring trade. The cacophony of squealing kids and loud music managed to drown out most of Reggie's melancholy thoughts. He felt drained. He had no idea how he was going to get through this performance. His mental energies were spent.

Gizelle rode over to where he was standing in the line.

"You ok mate?"

Reggie nodded but couldn't meet her eyes. He felt if he looked at her he would lose it completely.

Just as their strained silence almost reached tipping point, Treloar hurried over and had a quiet word with them both. Gizelle beamed and, giving Reggie a cheeky wink, trotted off to join her line. Treloar put one hand on Reggie's shoulder and, with a tight fist, gently knocked him on the chin with the other.

"You ready Trooper?" he asked.

Reggie couldn't speak. Tears welled in his eyes but he managed a crooked smile, and nodded.

"Good man!" said Treloar and strode away to the head of the line.

***

Reggie's second performance was a knockout, with Gizelle and Hunter shooing him along. The more they pushed him, the more he unfolded and the more he gave. Halfway through one particular routine, he stopped dead. Sitting in front of him in rows one and two was a group of thirteen people. The sight of them almost took his breath away. He stood there, mouth open, swaying from side to side, a bit like Cindy whenever she was tethered. Hunter gave a soft whinny and pawed the ring, bringing Reggie out of his stupor. Returning to character, he pantomimed counting them, throwing his hands in the air and counting again and again. Stepping over the barrier he shook hands with each and every one of them, with exaggerated aplomb, all of them shaking their heads and giggling with embarrassment. He then stood back and looked at the broader audience, miming with animated outstretched hands that these people were his people. The crowd erupted with cheers and applause as he jumped up and down for joy, spreading the soft sawdust with his clumpy boots all over the shoes of those in the front row. He then pulled out his great big polka-dot clown hanky and pretended to cry, blowing his nose with loud raspberries for effect. Little did the spectators realise his tears of joy were real. The noise was deafening. Overcome with emotion that his family was there, he bowed solemnly to his mum as he held out his hand. She stood, somewhat shyly, as Reggie took her in his arms and executed a funny little waltz. There wasn't a dry eye in the house.

***

The following day Treloar invited the entire team to a sundowner under the Big Top. They weren't treated to this type of socialising very often but everyone could feel an inexplicable energy around the invitation. Wine and nibbles were laid out and the team made the most of it. Reggie had never attended anything like this before and stood back, feeling totally out of place. Everyone seemed to know what to do, except him. Gizelle was talking to some of the girls when she noticed him standing aside, looking unsure.

"What's up Reggie?"

"Nuthin'. I've just never been to anything like this before."

"Well, that's ok. It's just a team get-together. Grab yourself a drink and something to eat before the vultures clean it all up. There'll be nothing left soon."

His hesitation was palpable.

"Do they have any soft drink? I've never drunk alcohol."

"Well come with me and we'll see what we can find."

Gizelle took him by the arm and walked him over to the tables.

Reggie found a Fanta and just as he cracked the can the Ringmaster moved to the centre of the arena, tapping his glass, seeking the team's attention.

"Thanks everyone for coming," he said in his booming voice. "It's good to see you all in a social situation for a change. As you well know we don't do this often but then we don't always get the opportunity because of our outside commitments." Treloar looked around the arena, seeming to pass his eyes over every individual.

"I've invited you here today, not as your Ringmaster, but speaking as Sam Treloar. I would like to honour one of you, whom you have all come to know and respect. We have someone here who deserves recognition, not because he's good at his job or outstanding in some professional sense, but because he's outstanding on a personal level. Recently I asked this person to take on a role that I knew he would feel uncomfortable with. I knew it would probably give him the threepenny bits! As much as he wanted to reject the offer, when push came to shove – and he was shoved," said Treloar, with a broad grin on his face, remembering the Strong Man pushing Reggie through the curtains on his first night, "he stumbled into it. Now, he may not have consciously acknowledged this to himself, but the Circus needed him for this role, and, like it or not, he managed to step up to it with a little help, I might add, from a clever horse and a wonderful friend. I would also like to add that, as most of you are aware, there was a robbery here a couple of days ago and I'm very pleased to advise the culprit has been apprehended. I don't wish to go into great detail other than to say the robbery appears to have been planned out of jealousy, to throw bad light onto one of our own."

As the speech was in progress and people twigged as to who Treloar was talking about, the team parted to reveal Reggie standing at the very back near the drink tables. Everyone was looking towards him, big smiles on their faces.

Treloar continued. "I would like to raise a toast to our new best Clown, Mr Reggie Downer."

The team cheered and raised their glasses.

"To Reggie Downer," they chorused in unison.

Reggie stood there stunned. With tears in her eyes Gizelle threw her arms around his neck and gave him the biggest hug.

"Reggie, you are such a placid and uncomplicated soul," said Treloar. "I've never met anyone quite like you. You haven't got a mean bone in your body. Just watching you and the way animals respond to you is not something you see every day. You've touched all our lives in a way that is commendable. You are a pleasure to work with and I'm so pleased you are part of this team."

Amid roars of appreciation, Treloar went on to say he had received numerous positive compliments about the gentle clown, from many members of the audience.

"This can only be a good thing from the circus's point of view. Reggie, we can't do without you! Thank you, from the bottom of our hearts."

When there was nothing left to eat or drink everyone began to quietly disperse. Some of them caught up with Reggie and were patting him on the back or shaking his hand, congratulating him. Poor Reggie was so shy he hardly knew how to respond, but managed broad smiles and nods of thanks. Treloar was quietly watching this and once Reggie was alone he beckoned him over. Jack, Stan and Jimmy were talking to Gizelle near the Big Top entrance. Treloar waved them over also. With the little group gathered, Treloar opened up.

"I haven't been able to catch you altogether as I've had a busy day but I have some good news which will be of interest. I confess Reggie and Gizelle already know some of it. The reason I told them last night was I knew it would give Reggie a lift prior to the show as I'm sure he needed it! I received a phone call from the police sergeant just before the Big Top opened. It appears Frank Knight was pulled over for drink driving outside of town late yesterday afternoon. The two constables decided to search his vehicle and surprise, surprise, they found drugs and equipment that actually belongs to the circus. They impounded his vehicle and he's currently in the lockup. He will appear before the Magistrate tomorrow.

Stan let out a long, slow whistle – Jimmy and Jack looked astonished, but relieved. Gizelle was clinging on to Reggie's arm. Treloar stood there with a broad grin creasing his face. Stan walked over to Reggie and held out his hand.

"Sorry mate. We were too hasty with our accusations and condemnations."

"Hear, hear," echoed Jack and Jimmy as they both slapped Reggie on the back and pumped his hand up and down. Their delight was infectious.

"Well," said Treloar, still grinning from ear to ear, "I just wanted you to be the first to know. I think you might all sleep a little easier tonight!"

***

The following day Reggie and Gizelle were enjoying a quiet moment, sitting on a hay bale in the shade quietly watching a trainer playing ball with the elephants. Reggie wasn't saying much, just sitting, not looking at anything in particular, his thoughts introspective.

"You ok Reggie?" Gizelle asked, looking at him sideways, conscious of his inward stare.

"Yeah, yeah, I'm ok. Just thinkin' 'bout yesterday and the day before. I didn't mean to make a fuss.

"You didn't make a fuss, you Dodo," she squealed. "Treloar was complimenting you for all your good work. You were amazing in the ring once you got going. Everyone loved it. You're a natural!"

"Ha! You're just sayin' that!"

"No I am NOT! You stepped into the role even though you were uncomfortable with it. Accept it for what it is. You were so gentle with that little girl on the first night. That's what everyone loved! And look at the performance you gave last night. You wore your heart on your sleeve!"

"Well, I would'na done it any other way."

"Exactly! That's why everyone loved it. I loved it! You showed them who you really are!"

A small, poignant silence flattened out between them.

"Will you stay with the circus?" Gizelle asked, quizzically. "We move on at the end of next week."

"Dunno. Not sure what to do. Feel a bit queer about it all."

"Why?"

"Dunno. I've never thought my life would amount to much. I just go with the flow. You know!"

"Oh my Lord! You are such a goose Reggie Downer. You've got something great staring you in the face and you're too dumb to see it!"

It was Reggie's turn to stare at Gizelle. A small battle was curling his thoughts, but he slowly let it unfurl.

"Ok, but before I make me mind up for good, I have a question."

"Shoot."

"Why do you always wear that black glove on your left arm?"

Gizelle stared at him. "Is that it? Whether you stay or not depends on if I answer your question?"

"Well, yeah. Kinda."

"Reggie Downer. I thought you were a simple soul, and then you come out with this crap! What's it to ya?"

"I just wanna know."

Gizelle giggled, tossing her curls and causing them to fly everywhere.

"You know something? One reason I like you so much is you take people as they are. Heaps of blokes would have asked me that question on first meeting me, and you've taken nearly three bleedin' weeks. You rock my soul, mate!"

Gizelle went on to explain she had been born with only one hand. Although this hadn't stopped her from doing anything, she was often conscious of people staring, so the glove gave her some *space,* if you like, around others. She removed the glove to show him a small, slightly withered stump close to what would have been her wrist. She had been fortunate to grow up with very supportive parents, who also had a love of horses. There was no impediment with her disability. She had been well-schooled in horsemanship. Over the years she had competed in several paraplegic international horse events including the Paraplegic Olympics, and won several medals.

Reggie sat there, taking it all in. He had never been exposed to anything like this and wasn't sure how to respond. As the silence lengthened, Gizelle began to lose patience.

"So now what? Have you nothing to say? What are you thinking?"

Reggie gave her a crooked smile and decided to spin it out for a bit.

"Oh, I dunno. Don't have much to say one way or the other."

"YOU would have to be one of THE most frustrating men I've ever met!"

"Nah. I'm just a bloke. Anyway, you told me a few minutes ago how much you liked me!"

"Ooh, Reggie Downer, I could clock you!"

Turning away from her, he let several seconds elapse until he said quietly, into the wind, "Yeah, I'll stay."

"What did you say? WHAT DID YOU JUST SAY?"

He turned and gave her a quick nod and a wink. "There's no need to yell," he said, as he put his arm around her shoulder and took the unprecedented step, for him, of brushing her cheek with his lips.

"I'll stay!"

Keep reading for a sneak Preview of,
Two Shakes of a Dead Lamb's Tail
Noreen Reeves' first volume of her memoirs.

Two Shakes of a Dead Lamb's Tail

It was a shotgun wedding and the Vicar's eyes popped out as I walked down the aisle leaning on my dad's arm. We hadn't disclosed our little indiscretion when making the church arrangements, and by the time the wedding took place I was almost five months pregnant.

John and I had met at a dance called *Power House* that was held every Sunday night at the Albert Park Lake Hall in Melbourne. It was a very popular venue and the girls would line up along the walls while the blokes walked past, eyeing us off like cattle in a saleyard. It was fairly demeaning standing there like a veritable wallflower hoping someone would ask you to dance. I was with a girlfriend and she beseeched me not to accept any more dances. She hadn't had one all night and I think she was feeling the pinch.

As the constant stream of males filed past, this very thin guy gave a quick, cheeky smile, cocked his head sideways and said, "Dance?" Off I went.

I have to confess that looking back, I remember the dance with some amusement. It was 1968 and *The Beatles* and *Rolling Stones* were in flavour. Judy Durham, before *The Seekers*, was also a hot item. I had quiet pride in that I could bop with the best of them, but watching John dance I stood there in disbelief as he ranged all over the dance floor, lost to the music. I had never seen anyone so uncoordinated. It was almost as though he didn't need a partner. I still have a quiet chuckle at the memory.

He drove me home in his mini and we sat outside chatting, when suddenly mum yelled out at the top of her voice, "Noreen, come inside!" Oh, the embarrassment! This wasn't the first time my parents had alerted the neighbourhood about my nocturnal arrivals.

John was a teacher, employed at Swan Hill Technical School and surprisingly he said he'd be in touch. Whenever he came to Melbourne we would go somewhere on a Saturday night, usually to a party with his college friends. These people really knew how to party! We went out together for several months, but stuff happens, as they say and although on occasions we had been close, full-blown sex never occurred.

Morning sickness began and initially I dismissed it as something I must have eaten, however, after many mornings my mum became concerned and very suspicious. She insisted I see the doctor. Doctor Collie had known me all my life and I was nearly always in fear and trepidation of him. Not that he was a bad doctor, he was very good and very thorough but my misgivings about seeing him on this occasion had me trembling. I don't remember the initial discussion but he knew enough from mum's information to send me off to a specialist for further consultation. The 'baby' word had been mentioned and I was in denial – telling myself I knew exactly how babies were made. It simply couldn't be.

There is something wonderful and at the same time terrible about naiveté and innocence. Wonderful, because innocence allows the gullible to see wonder in all its glory. Terrible, because it sometimes obstructs a harsh reality, blinding the naive to the truth.

I attended a specialist in East Melbourne and after an internal examination he confirmed I was pregnant. I cannot describe the emotions that flooded my addled brain. I lay there stunned, in total disbelief. He advised me he would inform Dr Collie and that I needed to refer back to him. Trying unsuccessfully to stem tears, on shaking legs I wobbled down the wide stone steps and out into the busy street, steadying myself on the sandstone fence pillar. It was late afternoon and traffic was at its peak. I couldn't breathe. I was hot. I was disoriented and in fear of going home. But where else could I go and be safe? I heard what the specialist said but my mind couldn't compute the information. This simply couldn't be true. Blood swirled behind my eyes in a vortex. I was so traumatised I didn't know what to do and I couldn't remember where I'd parked the car. How on earth was I going to concentrate driving home in peak hour traffic? I eventually found the car and sat there, frozen, terrified of the home consequences. Gripping the steering wheel, I sat there, shaking.

Knowing the music had to be faced, I joined the congested traffic. A young policeman was on point duty and I was hopeful of moving past him when his hand shot up to stop. This had me concerned. I had cried so much I knew I looked a mess and was hopeful he wouldn't notice. He did! He looked at me hard and motioned for me to speak but I shook my head and stared straight ahead. He in turn looked quite troubled, but eventually waved me on.

When I reached my home street, I sat parked at the kerb several houses away, out of sight. Fearful! My dad was a policeman and although I knew he loved me he was over protective to the point of suffocation. It was dad I was scared of and seriously afraid of his reaction.

I pulled into the driveway and there was dad, waiting. I almost wet my pants, so great was my fear. When I eventually found my legs and emerged from the car, he opened his arms. I fell into him sobbing. "The doctor said I'm pregnant and I don't know how." He held me tight and said I wasn't to worry, he would look after me. I couldn't believe my ears. I was expecting an explosion, not care and consideration. We stood there for many minutes but I knew I couldn't evade the inevitable. I had to go in and face mum.

Having been buoyed somewhat by dad's reaction, I wasn't prepared for mum's. She had no doubt been listening at the back door to what had been said. Her eyes were red-rimmed, and when I reached for her, she backed away and wouldn't look at me. This was a reaction I wasn't expecting, but I couldn't blame her. I had let her down – let them both down.

Dinner was a disaster. I couldn't eat so made my goodnights and went to bed. Sleep evaded me for hours, and when I did sleep, it was distracted and fitful. Next morning as I was leaving for work I went to kiss mum goodbye, but she turned her face away. I think, in hindsight, I could have stood dad's wrath. Mum's reaction cut me to the quick. I stumbled through the next few days and then, taking a deep breath, had to revisit Doctor Collie.

"How did it happen?" he asked, as he gently guided me into his office.

I almost laughed. If he didn't know, what was I doing there?

"I don't know doctor. I've never had intercourse," and added after a brief pause, "with anyone." Doctor and patient's eyes locked, one set with a sympathetic tenderness, the other set, moist, red and desperate in their appeal. The silence that ensued held both doctor and patient captive, like an unsevered umbilical cord between deliverer and deliveree.

For the next half-hour he gently guided me through the question and answer routine, saying he felt very sorry for me, as in his profession he saw many other girls caught in this unwanted situation – adding those girls got what they deserved. With the opening up of the discussion I became brave enough to ask how it could happen without penetration. He advised me that sperm, once released, only has to be on pubic hair, and they could find their way to the vagina. I was stunned and sat there in disbelief. He quietly added, "You have no idea how unlucky you are." He also advised that, from the specialist's report, it would be unwise to consider termination because although I wasn't sure of my dates, I was approximately four months pregnant. Shock waves hit me like a bomb blast. It was bad enough I was pregnant – I hadn't even considered termination.

On relaying the visit to my parents, my father almost had an apoplectic fit. "No grandchild of mine is going to be terminated," he roared, as he stomped around the kitchen in a near frenzied fit.

Dilemma number two was what was I to do? It wasn't going to take long before people realised my condition and I thought the embarrassment of the situation was going to destroy me.

The next few weeks saw me on a merry-go-round of discussions and decisions, but one aspect of this had me completely discombobulated. All the decisions being made about me were without me being included. They had me going *somewhere* in the country until I delivered, so no-one would know; the baby could perhaps be adopted. My father's reaction to this was – Like hell, I'm not going through the rest of my life not knowing my grandchild. So that sealed that argument! My eldest brother and his wife had two small children – maybe they could adopt the baby, and I could be 'aunty'. My reaction was also, Like hell! It wasn't that I wasn't grateful for their thoughts but how was I supposed to cope, visiting and seeing my child being brought up by someone else. The seesaw and the pendulum rose and swung to their own rhythms, and sometimes the near misses were too close for comfort.

And what about John? He hadn't, as yet, been told.

He arrived from Swan Hill one evening looking tired from a full week teaching and the long drive to Melbourne. He was to stay at our place. Mum and dad were walking a knife's edge. I tried covering my tension as there was no way I wanted John to pick up any disruptive vibes. I knew I had to tell him, and for most of the meal my heart was in my mouth. The poor bloke didn't know what he was walking into.

The night was warm and after doing the dishes I suggested we sit outside in the cool. Some small talk played out, but with my innards in a vice, I eventually said I had something to tell him. The silence was deafening. I wanted to cry but held my emotions in check and relayed everything that had happened. My most pressing question to him was, did he know pregnancy could happen that way? He was as confounded as me. Awkward situations are never comfortable, but I hastened to add that while marriage could be an option, I wasn't going to hold him to it if his feelings didn't run that way. Long silences ensued. One of his comments was regarding his parents. I knew his heart was bleeding.

"Looks like the blue-eyed boy isn't so blue-eyed after all," was all he could say.

John finally asked me how I felt about getting married. I said it would be ok but implored him to sleep on it. I didn't want him making any rash decisions, only to regret them. I was prepared to go through with the pregnancy and let the circumstances play out, but in no way did I want him to feel trapped.

The light in the sleep-out burned all night. I walked to and from the back door several times, my heart aching. I couldn't even begin to imagine what he was thinking or going through. Before retiring, mum had asked me the burning question. I felt strangely calm and reiterated what I had said to John – he needed time to think, and I wasn't going to pressure him. He had to make his own decision and I was prepared to accept his choice.

Breakfast came and went with some discomfort. We sat outside once more in the dry, sunny morning air and talked through many things. Finally a decision was made, and John left to visit his sister. He needed his family.

I went back inside. Mum was like 'a cat on a hot tin roof'. The suspense was killing her. After three weeks of almost no interaction with my mother (her choice) I was now in the driver's seat, and for a short time wasn't prepared to return to being the passenger. I have to confess there were a range of emotions flowing through my veins, most of them happy ones. The slide going down had finally tilted the other way.

With impish glee which was difficult to contain, I finally told mum we had agreed to get married. Now I think I missed something here! Suddenly my whole world changed. 'Amazing Grace' went into overdrive! That same day the cake was ordered; we had to go shopping for material for a dress; mum needed a new dress and was I going to have a bridesmaid? Corsages had to be ordered together with the men's buttonhole flowers. My bouquet would be an eleven-flower spike from one of mum's orchids. Where were we going to have the wedding reception? "Oh, by the way, you're not getting married at Benson Street. I don't want anyone down there knowing. John's Anglican, so you can get married at the Anglican Church in Union Road!" That's that then! There was an unmapped whirlwind in our house and I felt like I was being blown from pillar to post.

The next hurdle John and I both had to face was driving to north-eastern Victoria where his mother and father lived. Tungamah is roughly a three-hour drive from Melbourne and the closer we got, the quieter we both became. His parents weren't expecting us, so they were taken by surprise when we arrived. Pleasantries were exchanged and a cuppa made. I could feel John's tension escalating, as was mine. The reason for the visit was finally disclosed, and of course, there was deadly silence. I was choking back tears as I knew how much his parents were hurting, but to my dying day I will be eternally grateful to Jack, John's wonderful dad. He sat there for a little while thinking, and then turned to me with his smiling blue eyes and said, "Well, it looks like I've got myself a daughter-in-law."

The wedding took place three weeks later in November 1968 at the Anglican Church in Union Road, Surrey Hills, as decreed by mum. On the morning of the wedding, I was booked into the hairdressers for a shampoo and style. I had long blonde hair, almost waist length. Bouffant hairstyles were the fashion and the hairdresser went for it! By the time she had finished teasing and styling, I had the mane of a lion and looked like I had just escaped from the zoo. I ran home, mortified. As I reached the back door mum stepped out. She took one look at me and said, "You needn't think you're going to the church looking like that!" This tipped me over the edge. I tore into my bedroom and slammed what was, up until then, an un-slam-able door, threw myself on the bed and howled. With huge blobs for eyes, I spent the next hour trying to comb and brush the knots out and finally managed to tame the mane to something acceptable.

***

The wedding went off without a hitch. All was well as we exited the church except for one small hiccup. One of Benson Street's biggest gossips was standing outside. So much for mum's best laid plans!

Mum insisted on a small reception, so only uncles and aunties and just a few close friends were invited. A restaurant had been hired and although it was only a small party, the food and ambience were excellent. Everyone remarked it was one of the best weddings they had ever been to because it was so uncomplicated. The funniest and most endearing memory of that night, for me, was the meal and drinks for twenty people. The cost was only $90 and dad spent the rest of the evening trying to give the Restaurant Manager more money. He was sure the Manager had made a clerical error.

Our gorgeous son Andrew was born the following March.

***

I miss my mother. How I wish I could talk to her just one more time. But one more time wouldn't be enough, would it! My mother was one of the warmest and most generous people I have ever had the good fortune to know. She could be funny but also

159

as tough as nails, when required. She taught me a lot, and I am so grateful for her friendship and love, through good times and bad.

Pictures

Connie Falkiner
My best friend

**Bucket wheel changeout. Cape Lambert WA 2006
Me and Jeff Pas, site construction manager.**

Feed time - Me, Melanie and poddy lamb 1981

Melanie, Dylan and Andrew
My three kids!

Gallarus Oratory, Dingle, Ireland
700 - 1200 AD

A57A Iceberg, Antarctica, 2019
20km in length; 9km wide.
An Arab gent wanted to tow it to Arabia

**John and Tomas, Tinputz, Bougainville Is PNG 2019
Tomas was one of John's students in 1972**

Transport PNG style - 1971

My Country

About The Author

Noreen Reeves grew up in Melbourne, Australia. After marrying in 1968, she and her husband lived in country Victoria before embarking for Bougainville Island, Papua New Guinea, where they lived on an isolated outstation. While her husband worked as a teacher, Noreen occupied her time with raising three children and helping out where she could with the Vocational Centre.

On returning to Australia in 1973, the family lived in East Gippsland, Victoria, operating a wholesale native tree nursery as well as farming sheep and cattle, before buying a 101,250 hectare sheep station in outback Western Australia in 1985. During her career, Noreen also worked as an administrator for various companies, including accountants, solicitors, the Royal Agricultural Society of WA, a firm of German engineers and, by far her favourite, the Wine Industry Association of WA.

In 2016 she retired and finally was able to give time and attention to her writing. Having published her memoir, *"Two Shakes of a Dead Lamb's Tail"* in 2013, Noreen is enjoying retirement and looking forward to beginning work on a fiction novel.

Website: https://www.noreenreeves.com.au

Facebook: https://facebook.com/norzreeves

Acknowledgements

I wish to thank the following people for their encouragement and support, assistance, advice and suggestions, all of whom are, and always will be, greatly appreciated.

Lizzie McGovern for her critical and impartial eye when it came to punctuation, spelling and paragraphing.

Sally Boardman for her constant enthusiasm and encouragement.

Cheryl McMillan for being my best friend, my (sometimes) wisest critic and for all her wonderful suggestions and opinions when my thoughts ran dry.

Ian Hooper and the team at Leschenault Press for their assistance, advice and professionalism throughout.

Lindy Ferris – Editor extraordinaire! A huge thank you. I really enjoyed the process!

My family, for their support and humour, which I cannot live without.

To my friends and family who contributed to the stories, by being part of them.

And my friend Connie – I will always miss you!